ERLE STANLEY GARDNER

- Cited by the *Guinness Book of World Records* as the #1 best-selling writer of all time!

- Author of more than 150 clever, authentic, and sophisticated mystery novels!

- Creator of the amazing Perry Mason, the savvy Della Street, and dynamite detective Paul Drake!

- **THE ONLY AUTHOR WHO OUTSELLS AGATHA CHRISTIE, HAROLD ROBBINS, BARBARA CARTLAND, AND LOUIS L'AMOUR *COMBINED*!**

Why?

Because he writes the best, mo̶s̶t̶ ̶fa̶scinating whoduni̶t̶s̶

You'll ̶ ̶ ̶ ̶ ̶ ̶ ̶ ̶ ̶ ̶ ̶ ̶ ̶ ̶ ̶ ̶ ̶them,

Also by Erle Stanley Gardner
Published by Ballantine Books:

The Case of the
Terrified Typist

Erle Stanley Gardner

BALLANTINE BOOKS • NEW YORK

ISBN O-345-34165-1

This edition published by arrangement with William Morrow and
Company, Inc.

Manufactured in the United States of America

First Ballantine Books Edition: April 1987

CAST OF CHARACTERS

Foreword

It is so trite to say that truth is stranger than fiction that one dislikes to use the expression, yet there is absolutely no other way of describing the strange situation that took place in Texas, where within the framework of the law a principality was created that was completely foreign to all of our American traditions.

All of this started out innocently enough. A large section of Texas was peopled by Spanish-speaking citizens and an American acquired a position of leadership and started advising these people how to mark their ballots. Apparently he had their best interests at heart and received their virtually unanimous support.

The community became known as the Principality of Duval and the man who gave the instructions to the voters was known as the "Duke of Duval."

Later on this situation developed to a point where successors to the Duke of Duval used their power to establish what was in effect a principality within a state. That principality became steeped in hatreds and ruled by fear, and fear ruled with an iron hand.

The state seemed powerless. The whole machinery of government in Duval was in the hands of one person.

Then my friend the Honorable John Ben Shepperd became the attorney general of the State of Texas.

Shepperd went into Duval and started fighting.

It was a knockdown drag-out fight. The story of what happened is so lurid, so utterly inconceivable that it staggers the imagination.

John Ben Shepperd won that fight. It took courage, honesty, competence, resourcefulness and guts.

When I first knew John Ben Shepperd, he was the

attorney general of Texas. I am honored that he made me an honorary special assistant attorney general of Texas, and my commission as such hangs in my office today.

Texans don't do things the way other people do. If a Texan likes you, he is for you a hundred per cent. If he doesn't like you, he may or may not be polite, but his formal politeness will be as frigid as a blizzard wind in the Texas Panhandle.

Texas is a big, raw, blustering state with a highly developed sense of the dramatic, a spirit of the Old West still rampant, and is peopled by citizens who think only in terms of the superlative. This causes many people to doubt the sincerity of the Texan. The trouble is some of these critics simply don't understand the Texan language and the Texan thought. When a Texan uses superlatives, he is completely sincere. He thinks in superlatives. He expresses himself in superlatives.

On one of my recent trips to Texas, I was the speaker at a noonday banquet. My big plate tried in vain to hold a Texas-size steak which overflowed it at the edges.

As soon as that banquet was over, the chief of police rushed me out to his automobile and with red light and screaming siren, we started for the airport.

At the airport my friend the late Jim West, one of Texas' rugged multimillionaires, had his plane waiting and as soon as he heard the siren screaming in the distance, he started warming up the motors. By the time the police car speeded onto the airport's runway and stopped within a few feet of the airplane, the motors were warmed up and ready for a take-off.

I was rushed up into the interior of the plane, the door slammed, the motors roared and the plane was in the air.

An hour and a half later, almost an hour of which had been spent in flying over Jim West's ranch, we came down at the ranch house. A servant put a gallon flagon in my hand. It was filled with cold, frothy beer. As fast as I lowered the flagon an inch or so, someone would reach over my shoulder with a couple more cans of ice-cold beer and keep it up to the brim.

Shortly afterward we had a "little old barbecue." I was given a steak that was so big it had to be served on a platter.

When we had finished that repast, Jim West announced that his nearest neighbor, who lived thirty-odd miles away, wanted to meet our group and we were transported in specially made Jeeps to the ranch of Dolph Briscoe.

Briscoe greeted us with typical Texas hospitality. He invited us in for a "snack."

The snack consisted of—you guessed it. And Dolph Briscoe was properly apologetic.

"That steer," he said in his Texas drawl, "played me false. I tried to make him weigh a ton, but after he got up to nineteen hundred and sixty pounds he just wouldn't put on any more fat, and in order to have the meat properly aged for you folks when you got here, I had to kill him when he was just forty pounds short of a ton. I'm not going to lie to you folks, that there's a Texas steer but he's forty pounds short of a ton."

Now that's Texas. If you don't understand it, it seems weird and bizarre. If you understand it, you love it and you love the Texans, and your understanding has to be based on the fact that the underlying keynote of the Texan is sincerity. If he likes you, he wants to do everything he can for you.

There is the old story of the Texan who went out to lunch with his friend. After lunch the friend stopped in at a Cadillac agency to look over a new car he was thinking of buying.

When he finally made up his mind to buy the car, the Texan whipped out his checkbook. "Here," he said, "this one is on me. You paid for the lunch."

That story is probably an exaggeration, but it is nevertheless typical.

My friend John Ben Shepperd is a Texan. When he embarked upon a career of law enforcement as attorney general of Texas, he went all the way. Entirely at his own expense he published a newsletter roundup of crime and justice for the Lone Star State. He tried to see that all law enforcement officers knew what the law was.

As my friend the Honorable Park Street, a prominent trial

attorney of San Antonio and for years an associate of mine on the Court of Last Resort, expressed it, "Many a criminal is caught in Texas by a cowboy-booted constable or sheriff whose standard equipment includes a .45 revolver and a blue-backed *Peace Officer's Handbook*, written by John Ben Shepperd."

"Crime," drawls John Ben Shepperd, "is not sluggish or unintelligent. It plays infinite variations on its own theme, developing new forms and methods. Like the hare and the tortoise, it outruns us unless we plod relentlessly along carrying the law forward on our backs."

From time to time, I made talks on law enforcement in Texas while John Ben Shepperd was the attorney general of the state.

From the time my group arrived at the borders of Texas, we would be met by assistant attorneys general, airplanes and prominent citizens. We would be whisked from place to place at breath-taking schedule, yet the whole itinerary would be carefully planned to the last detail: Planes would be waiting for us at dawn, would take off on schedule and arrive on schedule for breakfast appointments and conferences. Lunches would be at points several hundred miles distant and we would be back in Austin for dinner. The pace was relentless and terrific. Yet the assistants assured me that this was the tempo at which John Ben Shepperd conducted his office.

Heaven knows how many honors were conferred upon him. I do know that he was the deserving recipient of three honorary Doctor of Laws degrees, and I also know that one of the honors he valued at the top of the list was a simple plaque presented to him by United Mothers and Wives of Duval County. It says, "To John Ben Shepperd, who purchased with courage and Christian integrity the right of our children to grow up uncorrupted and unafraid."

And so I dedicate this book to my friend—

THE HONORABLE JOHN BEN SHEPPERD

—Erle Stanley Gardner

Temecula, 1955

Chapter 1

Perry Mason eyed the brief which Jackson, his law clerk, had submitted for his approval.

Della Street, sitting across the desk from the lawyer, correctly interpreted the expression on Mason's face.

"What was wrong with it?" she asked.

"Quite a few things," Mason said. "In the first place, I've had to shorten it from ninety-six pages to thirty-two."

"Good heavens," Della said. "Jackson told me he had already shortened it twice and he couldn't take out another word."

Mason grinned. "How are we fixed for typists, Della?"

"Stella is down with the flu and Annie is simply snowed under an avalanche of work."

"Then we'll have to get an outside typist," Mason told her. "This brief has to be ready for the printer tomorrow."

"All right. I'll call the agency and have a typist sent up right away," Della Street promised.

"In the meantime," Mason told her, "I'm going over this thing once again and see if I can't take out another four or five pages. Briefs shouldn't be written to impress the client. They should be concise, and above all, the writer should see that the Court has a clear grasp of the *facts* in the case before there is any argument about the *law*. The judges know the law. If they don't, they have clerks who can look it up."

Mason picked up a thick blue pencil, held it poised in his hand, and once more started reading through the sheaf of pages, which already showed signs of heavy editing. Della Street went to the outer office to telephone for a typist.

When she returned Mason looked up. "Get one?"

"The agency doesn't have one at the moment. That is,

1

those they have are rather mediocre. I told them you wanted one who is fast, accurate and willing; that you didn't want to have to read this thing through again and find a lot of typographical errors."

Mason nodded, went on with his editing. "When can we expect one, Della?"

"They promised to have someone who would finish it by two-thirty tomorrow afternoon. But they said it might be a while before they could locate just the girl they wanted. I told them there were thirty-two pages."

"Twenty-nine and a half," Mason corrected, smilingly. "I've just cut out another two and a half pages."

Mason was just finishing his final editing half an hour later when Gertie, the office receptionist, opened the door and said, "The typist is here, Mr. Mason."

Mason nodded and stretched back in his chair. Della started to pick up the brief, but hesitated as Gertie came in and carefully closed the door behind her.

"What's the trouble, Gertie?"

"What did you say to frighten her, Mr. Mason?"

Mason glanced at Della Street.

"Heavens," Della said, "I didn't talk with *her* at all. We just rang up Miss Mosher at the agency."

"Well," Gertie said, lowering her voice, "this girl's scared to death."

Mason flashed a quick smile at Della Street. Gertie's tendency to romanticize and dramatize every situation was so well known that it was something of an office joke.

"What did *you* do to frighten her, Gertie?"

"*Me!* What did *I* do? Nothing! I was answering a call at the switchboard. When I turned around, this girl was standing there by the reception desk. I hadn't heard her come in. She tried to say something, but she could hardly talk. She just stood there. I didn't think so much of it at the time, but afterward, when I got to thinking it over, I realized that she was sort of holding on the desk. I'll bet her knees were weak and she—"

"Never mind what you thought," Mason interrupted,

puzzled. "Let's find out what happened, Gertie. What did you tell her?"

"I just said, 'I guess you're the new typist,' and she nodded. I said, 'Well, you sit over at that desk and I'll get the work for you.'"

"And what did she do?"

"She went over to the chair and sat down at the desk."

Mason said, "All right, Gertie. Thanks for telling us."

"She's absolutely terrified," Gertie insisted.

"Well, that's fine," Mason said. "Some girls are that way when they're starting on a new job. As I remember, Gertie, *you* had *your* troubles when you first came here, didn't you?"

"Troubles!" Gertie exclaimed. "Mr. Mason, after I got in the office and realized I'd forgotten to take the gum out of my mouth, I was just absolutely gone. I turned to jelly. I didn't know what to do. I—"

"Well, get back to the board," Mason told her. "I think I can hear it buzzing from here."

"Oh Lord, yes," Gertie said. "I can hear it now myself."

She jerked open the door and made a dash for the switchboard in the outer office.

Mason handed Della Street the brief and said, "Go out and get her started, Della."

When Della Street came back at the end of ten minutes Mason asked, "How's our terrified typist, Della?"

Della Street said, "If that's a terrified typist, let's call Miss Mosher and tell her to frighten all of them before sending them out."

"Good?" Mason asked.

"Listen," Della Street said.

She eased open the door to the outer office. The sound of clattering typewriter keys came through in a steady staccato.

"Sounds like hail on a tin roof," Mason said.

Della Street closed the door. "I've never seen anything like it. That girl pulled the typewriter over to her, ratcheted in the paper, looked at the copy, put her hands over the keyboard and that typewriter literally exploded into action. And yet, somehow, Chief, I think Gertie *was* right. I think she became frightened at the idea of coming up here. It may be that she knows something about you, or your fame has caused her to become self-conscious. After all," Della Street added dryly, "you're not entirely unknown, you know."

"Well," Mason said, "let's get at that pile of mail and skim off a few of the important letters. At that rate the brief will be done in plenty of time."

Della Street nodded.

"You have her at the desk by the door to the law library?"

"That seemed to be the only place to put her, Chief. I fixed up the desk there when I knew we were going to need an extra typist. You know how Stella is about anyone using *her* typewriter. She thinks a strange typist throws it all out of kilter."

Mason nodded, said, "If this girl is good, Della, you might arrange to keep her on for a week or two. We can keep her busy, can't we?"

"I'll say."

"Better ring up Miss Mosher and tell her."

Della Street hesitated. "Would it be all right if we waited until we've had a chance to study her work? She's fast, all right, but we'd better be sure she's accurate."

Mason nodded, said, "Good idea, Della. Let's wait and see."

Chapter 2

Della Street placed a sheaf of pages on Mason's desk. "Those are the first ten pages of the brief, Chief."

Mason looked at the typewritten sheets, gave a low whistle and said, "Now *that's* what I call typing!"

Della Street picked up one of the pages, tilted it so that the light reflected from the smooth surface. "I've tried this with two or three sheets," she said, "and I can't see where there's been a single erasure. She has a wonderful touch and she certainly is hammering it out."

Mason said, "Ring up Miss Mosher. Find out something about this girl. What's her name, Della?"

"Mae Wallis."

"Get Miss Mosher on the line."

Della Street picked up the telephone, said to Gertie at the switchboard, "Mr. Mason wants Miss Mosher at the secretarial agency, Gertie. . . . Never mind, I'll hold the line."

A moment later Della Street said, "Hello, Miss Mosher? . . . Oh, she is? . . . Well, I'm calling about the typist she sent up to Mr. Mason's office. This is Della Street, Mr. Mason's secretary. . . . Are you sure? . . . Well, she must have left a note somewhere. . . . Yes, yes . . . well, I'm sorry. . . . No, we don't want *two* girls . . . . No, no. Miss Mosher sent one up—a Mae Wallis. I'm trying to find out whether she'll be available for steady work during the next week. . . . Please ask Miss Mosher to call when she comes in."

Della Street hung up the phone, turned to Perry Mason. "Miss Mosher is out. The girl she left in charge doesn't know about anyone having been sent up. She found a note on the desk to get us a typist. It was a memo Miss Mosher left before she went out. The names of three girls were on it, and this assistant has been trying to locate the girls. One of them was laid up with flu, another one was on a job, and she was trying to locate the third when I called in."

"That's not like Miss Mosher," Mason said. "She's usually very efficient. When she sent this girl up, she should have destroyed the memo. Oh, well, it doesn't make any difference."

"Miss Mosher's due back in about an hour," Della Street said. "I left word for her to call when she comes in."

Again Mason tackled the work on his desk, stopping to see a client who had a three-thirty appointment, then returning to dictation.

At four-thirty Della Street went out to the outer office, came back and said, "She's still going like a house afire, Chief. She's really pounding them out."

Mason said, "That copy had been pretty badly hashed up and blue-penciled with strike-outs and interlineations."

"It doesn't seem to bother her a bit," Della Street said. "There's lightning in that girl's finger tips. She—"

The telephone on Della Street's desk shrilled insistently. Della Street, with her hand on the receiver, finished the sentence, ". . . certainly knows how to play a tune on a keyboard."

She picked up the receiver, said, "Hello. . . . Oh, yes, Miss Mosher. We were calling about the typist you sent up. . . . What? . . . You didn't? . . . Mae Wallis? . . . She *said* she came from your agency. She said you sent her. . . . Why, yes, that's what I understood she said. . . . Well, I'm sorry, Miss Mosher. There's been some mistake—but this girl's certainly competent. . . . Why, yes, she's got the work almost finished. I'm terribly sorry, I'll speak with her and—Are you going to be there for a while? . . . Well, I'll speak with her and call you back. But that's what she said . . . yes, from your agency . . . . All right, let me call you back."

Della Street dropped the phone into its cradle.

"Mystery?" Mason asked.

"I'll say. Miss Mosher says *she* hasn't sent anyone up. She's had a hard time getting girls lined up, particularly ones with qualifications to suit you."

"Well, she got one this time," Mason said, fingering through the brief. "Or at least *someone* got her."

"So what do we do?" Della Street asked.

"By all means, find out where she came from. Are you sure she said Miss Mosher sent her?"

"That's what Gertie said."

"Are you," Mason asked, "going *entirely* on what Gertie said?"

Della Street nodded.

"You didn't talk it over with Miss Wallis?"

"No. She was out there waiting to go to work. While I was talking with you, she found where the paper and carbons were kept in the desk. She'd ratcheted them into the machine, and just held out her hand for the copy. She asked if I wanted an original and three carbons. I said that we only used an original and two for stuff that was going to the printer. She said she had one extra carbon in the machine, but that she wouldn't bother to take it out. She said that she'd only make an original and two on the next. Then she put the papers down on the desk, held her fingers poised over the keyboard for a second, then started banging out copy."

"Permit me," Mason said, "to call your attention to something which clearly demonstrates the fallacy of human testimony. You were doubtless sincere in telling Miss Mosher that Mae Wallis said she had been sent up from her agency, but if you will recall Gertie's exact words, you will remember that she said the girl seemed frightened and self-conscious, so Gertie asked her if she was the new typist. The girl nodded, and Gertie showed her to the desk. At no time did Gertie say to us that she asked her if Miss Mosher had sent her."

"Well," Della Street said, "I had the distinct impression—"

"Certainly you did," Mason said. "So did I. Only long years of cross-examining witnesses have trained me to listen carefully to what a person actually says. I am quite certain that Gertie never told us she had specifically asked this girl if she came from Miss Mosher's agency."

"Well, where *could* she have come from?"

"Let's get her in and ask her," Mason said. "And let's not let her get away, Della. I'd like to catch up on some of this back work tomorrow, and this girl is really a wonder."

Della Street nodded, left her desk, went to the outer office, returned in a moment and made motions of powdering her nose.

"Did you leave word?" Mason asked.

"Yes, I told Gertie to send her in as soon as she came back."

"How's the brief coming?"

Della Street said, "She's well along with it. The work's on her desk. It hasn't been separated yet. The originals and carbons are together. She certainly does neat work, doesn't she?"

Mason nodded, tilted back in his swivel chair, lit a cigarette and said, "Well, we'll wait until she shows up and see what she has to say for herself, Della. When you stop to think about this, it presents an intriguing problem."

After Mason had smoked a leisurely cigarette Della Street once more went to the outer office and again returned.

Mason frowned, said, "She's probably one of those high-strung girls who use up a lot of nervous energy banging away at the typewriter and then go for a complete rest, smoking a cigarette or . . ."

"Or?" Della Street asked, as Mason paused.

". . . or taking a drink. Now, wait a minute, Della. Although there's nothing particularly confidential about that brief, if we keep her on here for four or five days, she's going to be doing some stuff that *is* confidential. Suppose you slip down to the powder room, Della, and see if perhaps our demon typist has a little flask in her purse and is now engaged in chewing on a clove."

"Also," Della Street said, "I'll take a whiff to see if I smell marijuana smoke."

"Know it when you smell it?" Mason asked, smiling.

"Of course," she retorted. "I wouldn't be working for one of the greatest trial attorneys in the country without having learned at least to recognize some of the more common forms of law violation."

"All right," Mason said. "Go on down and tell her that we want to see her, Della. Try and chat with her informally for a minute and size her up a bit. You didn't talk with her very much, did you?"

"Just got her name, and that's about all. I remember asking her how she spelled her first name, and she told me M-A-E."

Mason nodded. Della Street left the room and was back within a couple of minutes.

"She isn't there, Chief."

"Well, where the devil *is* she?" Mason asked.

Della Street shrugged her shoulders. "She just got up and went out."

"Say anything to Gertie about where she was going?"

"Not a word. She just got up and walked out, and Gertie assumed she was going to the washroom."

"Now that's strange," Mason said. "Isn't that room kept locked?"

"Della Street nodded.

"She should have asked for a key," Mason said. "Even if she didn't know it was locked, she'd have asked Gertie how to find it. How about her hat and coat?"

"Apparently she wasn't wearing any. She has her purse with her."

"Run out and pick up the last of the work she was doing, will you, Della? Let's take a look at it."

Della Street went out and returned with the typed pages. Mason looked them over.

"She has a few pages to go," Della Street said.

Mason pursed his lips, said, "It shouldn't take her long, Della, I certainly cut the insides out of those last few pages. That's where Jackson was waxing eloquent, bombarding the Court with a peroration on liberties, constitutional rights and due process of law."

"He was so proud of that," Della Street said. "You didn't take it *all* out, did you?"

"I took out most of it," Mason said. "An appellate court isn't interested in eloquence. It's interested in the law and the facts to which it is going to apply the law.

"Good Lord, Della, do you realize that if that appellate judges tried to read every line of all the briefs that are submitted to them, they could work for twelve hours each day without doing one other thing, and still couldn't read the briefs?"

"Good heavens, no! Aren't they supposed to read them?"

"Theoretically, yes," Mason said. "But actually, it's a practical impossibility."

"So what do they do?"

"Most of them look through the briefs, get the law points, skip the impassioned pleas, then turn the briefs over to their law clerks.

"It's my experience that a man does a lot better when he sets forth an absolutely impartial, thoroughly honest statement of facts, including those that are unfavorable to his side as well as those that are favorable, thus giving the appellate court the courtesy of assuming the judge knows the law.

"The attorney can be of help in letting the judge know the case to which the law is to be applied and the facts in the case. But if the judge didn't know what the law was, he wouldn't have been placed on the appellate bench in the first place. Della, what the devil *do* you suppose happened to that girl?"

"She must be in the building somewhere."

"What makes you think so?"

"Well, there again—well, it's just one of those presumptions. She certainly is coming back for her money. She put in a whale of an afternoon's work."

"She should have stayed to finish the brief," Mason said. "It wouldn't have taken her over another forty or fifty minutes, at the rate she was working."

"Chief," Della Street said, "you seem to be acting on the assumption that she's walked out and left us."

"It's a feeling I have."

Della Street said, "She probably went down to the cigar counter to buy some cigarettes."

"In which event, she'd have been back long before this."

"Yes, I suppose so. But . . . but, Chief, she's bound to collect the money for the work she's done."

Mason carefully arranged the pages of the brief. "Well, she's helped us out of quite a hole." He broke off as a series of peculiarly spaced knocks sounded on the corridor door of his private office.

"That will be Paul Drake," Mason said. "I wonder what brings *him* around. Let him in, Della."

Della Street opened the door. Paul Drake, head of the Drake Detective Agency, with offices down the corridor by the elevator, grinned at them and said, "What were *you* people doing during all of the excitement?"

"Excitement?" Mason asked.

"Cops crawling all over the building," Drake said. "And you two sitting here engaged in the prosaic activities of running a humdrum law office."

"Darned if we weren't," Mason said. "Sit down, Paul. Have a cigarette. Tell us what it's all about. We've been putting in our time writing briefs."

"You would," Drake told him, sliding down into the big overstuffed chair reserved for clients, and lighting a cigarette.

"What's the trouble?" Mason asked.

"Police chasing some dame up here on this floor," Drake said. "Didn't they search your office?"

Mason flashed a swift, warning glance at Della Street.

"Not that I know of."

"They must have."

Mason said to Della Street, "See if Gertie's gone home, Della."

Della Street opened the door to the outer office, said, "She's just going home, Chief."

"Can you catch her?"

"Sure. She's just at the door." Della Street raised her voice. "Oh, Gertie! Can you look in here for a minute?"

Gertie, ready to leave for the evening, came to stand in the doorway of the office. "What is it, Mr. Mason?"

"Any officers in here this afternoon?" Mason asked.

"Oh, yes," Gertie said. "There was some sort of a burglary down the corridor."

Again Mason caught Della's eye.

"What did they want?" Mason asked.

"Wanted to know if everyone in the office was accounted for, whether you had anyone in with you, and whether we had seen anything of a girl burglar."

"And what did you tell them?" Mason asked, keeping his voice entirely without expression.

"I told them you were alone, except for Miss Street, your confidential secretary. That we only had the regular employees here in the office and a relief typist from our regular agency who was working on a brief."

"And then what?"

"Then they left. Why?"

"Oh, nothing," Mason said. "I was just wondering, that's all."

"Should I have notified you? I know you don't like to be disturbed when you're working on correspondence."

"No, it's all right," Mason said. "I just wanted to get it straight, Gertie. That's all. Good night, and have a good time."

"How did you know I have a date?" Gertie asked.

"I saw it in your eyes," Mason said, grinning. "Good night, Gertie."

"Good night," she said.

12

"Well," Drake said, "there you are. If you'd happened to have had some woman client in your private office, the police would have insisted on talking to you and on getting a look at the client."

"You mean they searched the floor?" Mason asked.

"They really went through the joint," Drake told him. "You see, the office where the trouble occurred is right across from the women's restroom. One of the stenographers, opening the restroom door, saw this young woman whose back was toward her fumbling with the lock on the office door, trying first one key then another.

"The stenographer became suspicious. She stood there watching. About the fourth or fifth key, the girl managed to get into the office."

"What office was it?" Mason asked.

"The South African Gem Importing and Exploration Company."

"Go on, Paul."

"Well, this stenographer was a pretty smart babe. She telephoned the manager of the building and then she went out to stand by the elevators to see if this girl would come out and take an elevator. If she did that, the stenographer had made up her mind she'd try to follow."

"That could have been dangerous," Mason said.

"I know, but this is one very spunky gal."

"She could have recognized the woman?"

"Not the woman. But she knew the way the woman was dressed. You know the way women are, Perry. She hadn't seen the woman's face, but she knew the exact color and cut of her skirt and jacket, the shade of her stockings and shoes; the way she had her hair done, the color of her hair, and all that."

"I see," Mason said, glancing surreptitiously at Della Street. "That description was, of course, given to the police?"

"Oh, yes."

"And they didn't find her?"

"No, they didn't find a thing. But the manager of the

13

building gave them a passkey to get into the office of the gem importing company. The place looked as if a cyclone had struck it. Evidently, this girl had made a very hurried search. Drawers had been pulled out, papers dumped out on the floor, a chair had been overturned, a typewriter stand upset, with the typewriter lying on its side on the floor."

"No sign of the girl?"

"No sign of anyone. The two partners who own the business, chaps named Jefferson and Irving, came in right on the heels of the police. They had been out to lunch, and they were amazed to find how much destruction had taken place during their brief absence."

Mason said, "The girl probably ran down the stairs to another floor and took the elevator from there."

Drake shook his head. "The building manager got this stenographer who had given the description, and they went down to stand at the elevators. They watched everyone who went out. When the police showed up—and believe me, that was only a matter of a minute or two; these radio cars are right on the job—well, when the police showed up, the manager of the building briefed them on what had happened. So the police went up and the girl and the manager continued to stand at the elevators. The police weren't conspicuous about it, but they dropped in at every office on the floor, just checking up."

"And I suppose the restrooms," Mason said.

"Oh, sure. They sent a couple of girls into the restrooms right away. That was the first place they looked."

"Well," Mason said, "we seem to be doing all right, Paul. If I don't go out and get tangled up in crime, crime comes to me—at least indirectly. So Jefferson and Irving came in right after the police arrived, is that right?"

"That's right."

"And the manager of the building was down there at the elevators, waiting for this girl to come out?"

"That's right."

Mason said, "He knew, of course, the office that the girl was burglarizing?"

"Of course. He told the police what office it was and all about it. He even gave them a passkey so they could get in."

"And then he waited down there at the elevators with the stenographer who had seen this woman burglarizing the office?"

"That's right."

"A lot of elaborate precautions to catch a sneak thief."

"Well, I'm not supposed to talk about clients, Perry, and I wouldn't to anyone else, but as you know, I represent the owners of the building. It seems this gem importing company is expecting half a million dollars' worth of diamonds before long."

"The deuce!"

"That's right. You know the way they do things these days—insure 'em and ship 'em by mail."

"The strange thing," Mason said thoughtfully, "is that if Irving and Jefferson came in right on the heels of the police, with the manager of the building standing down there at the elevators, he didn't stop them and tell them that they'd find police in their office and—"

"What's the matter?" Mason asked, as Drake suddenly sat bolt upright.

Drake made the motion of hitting himself on the head.

"What are you trying to do?" Mason asked.

"Knock some brains into my thick skull," Drake said. "Good Lord, Perry! The manager of the building was telling me all about this, and that point never occurred to me. Let me use the phone."

Drake moved over to the phone, called the office of the manager and said, "Paul Drake talking. I was thinking about this trouble down at the gem importing company. According to police, Irving and Jefferson, the two partners who run the place, came in while they were searching."

The receiver made squawking noises.

"Well," Drake said, "*you* were standing down at the foot of the elevators with this stenographer. Why didn't you tell them that police were in their office—" Drake was interrupted by another series of squawking noises from the receiver. After a moment the detective said, "Want me to look into it, or do you want to? . . . Okay. Call me back, will you? I'm up here in Perry Mason's office at the moment. . . . Well, wait a minute. The switchboard is disconnected for the night, I guess. I'll catch that call at my—"

"Hold it, Paul," Della Street interrupted. "I'll connect this line with the switchboard, so you can get a call back on this number."

"Okay," Drake said into the telephone. "Mason's secretary will fix the line, so this telephone will be connected on the main trunk line. Just give me a buzz when you find out about it, will you?"

Drake hung up the telephone, went back to the client's chair, grinned at Mason and said, "You'll pardon me for taking all the credit for your idea, Perry, but this is my bread and butter. I couldn't tell him the idea never occurred to me until I got to talking with you, could I?"

"No credit," Mason said. "The thing is obvious."

"Of course it's obvious," Drake said. "That's why I'm kicking myself for not thinking of it right at the start. The trouble was, we were so interested in finding out how this girl vanished into thin air that I for one completely overlooked wondering how it happened that the manager didn't stop Jefferson and his partner and tell them what was happening."

"The manager was probably excited," Mason said.

"I'll tell the world he was excited. Do you know him?"

"Not the new one. I've talked with him on the phone, and Della Street's talked with him. I haven't met him."

"He's an excitable chap. One of those hair-triggered guys who does everything right now. At that, he did a pretty good job of sewing up the building."

Mason nodded. "They certainly went to a lot of trouble trying to catch one lone female prowler."

The telephone rang.

"That's probably for you," Della Street said, nodding to Paul Drake.

Drake picked up the telephone, said, "Hello. . . . Yes, this is Paul Drake. . . . Oh, I see. Well, of course, that could have happened, all right. Funny you didn't see them. . . . I see. Well, thanks a lot. I just thought we ought to check on that angle. . . . Oh, that's all right. There's no reason why that *should* have occurred to you. . . . Not at all. I'd been intending to ask you about it, but it slipped my mind. I thought I'd better check up on it before knocking off for the night. . . . Okay. Thanks. We'll see what we can find out."

Drake hung up, grinned at Mason and said, "Now the guy thinks I was working overtime, cudgeling my brain on his problem."

"What about the two partners?" Mason asked. "What's the answer?"

"Why, they evidently walked right by him and got in the elevator. Of course, the manager and the stenographer were watching the people who were getting *out* of the elevators. At that time, right after lunch, there's quite a bit of traffic in the elevators.

"The manager just finished talking with Jefferson on the phone. Jefferson said *he* saw the manager and this girl standing there and started to ask him a question about something pertaining to the building. Then he saw from the way the man was standing that he was evidently waiting for someone, so the two partners just went on past and got in the elevator just as it was starting up."

Mason said, "That sounds plausible, all right. What do you know about Jefferson and Irving? Anything?"

"Not too much. The South African Gem Importing and Exploration Company decided to open an office here. Their business is mostly wholesale diamonds. They have their main office in Johannesburg, but there's a branch office in Paris.

"This deal was made through the Paris office. They wrote the manager of the building, received a floor plan and rental

17

schedules, signed a lease and paid six months' rent in advance.

"They sent Duane Jefferson out from South Africa. He's to be in charge. Walter Irving came from the Paris office. He's the assistant."

"Are they doing business?"

"Not yet. They're just getting started. I understand they're waiting for a high-class burglarproof safe to be installed. They've advertised for office help and have purchased some office furniture."

"Did those two chaps bring any stock of diamonds with them?" Mason asked.

"Nope. Unfortunately, things aren't done that way any more, which has cost us private detectives a lot of business. Gems are sent by insured mail now. A half a million dollars' worth of stones are sent just as you'd send a package of soiled clothes. The shipper pays a fee for adequate insurance and deducts it as a business cost. If gems are lost, the insurance company writes out its check. It's an infallible, foolproof system."

"I see," Mason said thoughtfully. "In that case, what the devil was this girl after?"

"That's the sixty-four dollar question."

"It was an empty office—as far as gems go?"

"That's right. Later on, when the first shipment of gems arrives, they'll have burglar alarms all over the place, an impregnable safe and all the trimmings. Right now it's an empty shell.

"Gosh, Perry, it used to be that a messenger would carry a shipment of jewels, and private detective agencies would be given jobs as bodyguards, special watchmen and all of that. Now, some postal employee who doesn't even carry a gun comes down the corridor with a package worth half a million, says, 'Sign here,' and the birds sign their name, toss the package in the safe and that's all there is to it.

"It's all done on a basis of percentages. The insurance business is tough competition. How'd you like it if an insurance company would insure your clients against any loss from any type of litigation? Then your clients would pay premiums, deduct them as a business cost, and—"

"The trouble with that, Paul," Mason said, "is that when they come to lock a guy in the gas chamber it would take an awful big insurance check to make him feel indifferent."

Drake grinned. "Damned if it wouldn't," he agreed.

Chapter 3

When Paul Drake had left the office Mason turned to Della Street.

"Well, what do *you* think, Della?"

Della Street said, "I'm afraid it could be—it was about the same time and . . . well, sometimes I think we don't pay enough attention to Gertie because she *does* exaggerate. Perhaps this girl really was frightened, just as Gertie said, and . . . well, it could have been."

"Then she must have come in here," Mason said, "because she knew her escape was cut off. There was no other place for her to go. She had to enter some office. So she came in here blind and was trying to think of some problem that would enable her to ask for a consultation with me, when Gertie let the cat out of the bag that we were expecting a typist.

Della Street nodded.

"Go out and look around," Mason said. "I'm going out and do a little scouting myself."

"What do you want me to do?" Della Street asked.

"Look over the typewriter she was using. Look over the typewriter desk. Then go down to the restroom and look around. See if you can find anything."

"Heavens, the police have been all through the restroom."

"Look around, anyhow, Della. See if she hid anything. There's always the chance she might have had something in her possession that was pretty hot and she decided to cache it someplace and come back for it later. I'll go down and get some cigarettes."

Mason walked down the corridor and rang for an

elevator, went down to the foyer and over to the cigar stand. The girl behind the counter, a tall blonde with frosty blue eyes, smiled impersonally.

"Hello," Mason said.

At the personal approach the eyes became even more coldly cautious. "Good afternoon," the girl said.

"I am looking for a little information," Mason said.

"We sell cigars and cigarettes, chewing gum, candy, newspapers and magazines."

Mason laughed. "Well, don't get me wrong."

"And don't get *me* wrong."

"I'm a tenant in the building," Mason said, "and have been for some time. You're new here, aren't you?"

"Yes, I bought the cigar stand from Mr. Carson. I—Oh, I place you now! You're Perry Mason, the famous lawyer! Excuse me, Mr. Mason. I thought you were . . . well, you know a lot of people think that just because a girl is running a cigar counter she wraps herself up with every package of cigarettes she sells."

Mason smiled. "Pardon *me*. I should have introduced myself first."

"What can I do for you, Mr. Mason?"

"Probably nothing," Mason said. "I wanted a little information, but if you're new here, I'm afraid you won't know the tenants in the building well enough to help me."

"I'm afraid that's right, Mr. Mason. I don't have too good a memory for names and faces. I'm trying to get to know the regular customers. It's quite a job."

Mason said, "There are a couple of relative newcomers here in the building. One of them is named Jefferson, the other Irving."

"Oh, you mean the ones that have that gem importing company?"

"Those are the ones. Know them?"

"I do *now*. We had a lot of excitement here this afternoon, although I didn't know anything about it. It seems their office was broken into and—"

"They were pointed out to you?"

"Yes. One of them—Mr. Jefferson, I believe it was— stopped here for a package of cigarettes and was telling me all about it."

"But you didn't know them before?"

"You mean by sight?"

Mason nodded.

She shook her head. "I'm sorry, I can't help you, Mr. Mason."

"Well, that's all right," Mason told her.

"Why do you ask, Mr. Mason? Are you interested in the case?"

Mason smiled. "Indirectly," he said.

"You're *so* mysterious. I may not have recognized you when you walked up, but I have heard so much about you that I feel I know you very well indeed. What's an indirect interest, Mr. Mason?"

"Nothing worth talking about."

"Well, remember that I'm rather centrally located down here. If I can ever pick up any information for you, all you have to do is to let me know. I'll be glad to co-operate in any way that I can. Perhaps I can't be so efficient now, since I am relatively new here, but I'll get people spotted and . . . well, just remember, if there's *anything* I can do, I'll be glad to."

"Thanks," Mason told her.

"Did you want me to talk with Mr. Jefferson some more? He was quite friendly and chatted away with me while I was waiting on him. I didn't encourage him, but I have a feeling . . . well, you know how those things are, Mr. Mason."

Mason grinned. "You mean that he's lonely and he likes your looks?"

Her laugh showed that she was flustered. "Well, I didn't exactly say that."

"But you feel he could be encouraged?"

"Do you want me to try?"

"Would you like to?"

"Whatever you say, Mr. Mason."

The lawyer handed her a folded twenty dollar bill. "Try and find out just where the manager of the building was when Jefferson and Irving came back from lunch."

"Thank *you*, Mr. Mason. I feel guilty taking this money, because now that you mention the manager of the building I know the answer."

"What is it?"

"They came in while the manager and a young woman were standing watching the elevators. One of the men started to approach the manager as though he wanted to ask him a question, but he saw the manager was preoccupied watching the elevators, so he veered off.

"I didn't think anything about it at the time, but it comes back to me now that those were the two men who were pointed out to me later. I hope that's the information you wanted, Mr. Mason."

"It is, thanks."

"Thank *you*, Mr. Mason. If there's ever anything I can do for you I'd be glad to, and it isn't going to cost you a twenty every time either."

"Thanks," Mason said, "but I never want something for nothing."

"*You* wouldn't," she said, giving him her most dazzling smile.

Mason rode back up in the elevator.

Della Street, in a state of subdued excitement, was waiting to pounce on him as soon as he opened the door of his private office.

"Good heavens!" she said. "We're mixed in it up to our eyebrows."

"Go on," Mason said. "What are we mixed in?"

Della Street produced a small, square tin box.

"What," Mason asked, "do you have there?"

"A great big hunk of semi-dried chewing gum."

"And where did you get it?"

"It was plastered on the underside of the desk where Mae Willis had been working."

"Let's take a look, Della."

Della Street slid open the lid of the box and showed Mason the chewing gum. "This is just the way it was plastered to the underside of the desk," she said.

"And what did you do?"

"Took an old safety razor blade and cut it off. You can see there is an impression of fingers where she pushed the gum up against the desk."

Mason looked at Della Street somewhat quizzically. "Well," he said, "you *are* becoming the demon detective, Della. So now we have a couple of fingerprints?"

"Exactly."

"Well," Mason told her, "we're hardly going to the police with them, Della."

"No, I suppose not."

"So in that case, since we aren't particularly anxious to co-operate with the police, it would have been just as well if you had destroyed the fingerprints in removing the gum, Della."

"Wait," she told him. "You haven't seen anything yet. You observe that that's a terrific wad of gum, Chief. A girl could hardly have had all that in her mouth at one time."

"You think it was put there in installments?" Mason asked.

"I think it was put there for a purpose," Della Street said. "I thought so as soon as I saw it."

"What purpose?" Mason asked.

Della Street turned the box over on Mason's desk so that the wad of gum fell out on the blotter. "This," she said, "is the side that was against the desk."

Mason looked at the coruscations which gleamed through a few places in the chewing gum. "Good Lord, Della!" he said. "How many are there?"

"I don't know," Della said. "I didn't want to touch it. This is just the way it came from the desk. You can see parts of two really large-sized diamonds there."

Mason studied the wad of chewing gum.

"Now then," he said thoughtfully, "this becomes evidence, Della. We're going to have to be careful that nothing happens to it."

She nodded.

"I take it the gum is hard enough so it will keep all right?" Mason asked.

"It's a little soft on the inside, but now that the air's getting to the top, the gum is hardening rapidly."

Mason took the small tin box, replaced the gum and studied it, tilting the box backwards and forwards so as to get a good view of both the top and bottom sides of the chewing gum. "Two of those fingerprints are remarkably good latents, Della," he said. "The third one isn't so good. It looks more like the side of the finger. But those two impressions are perfect."

Della Street nodded.

"Probably the thumb and the forefinger. Which side of the desk was it on, Della?"

"Over on the right-hand side of the desk."

"Then those are probably the impressions of the right thumb and forefinger."

"So what do we do?" Della Street asked. "Do we now call in the police?"

Mason hesitated a moment, said, "I want to know a little more about what's cooking, Della. You didn't find anything in the restroom?"

Della Street said, "I became a scavenger. I dug down into the container that they use for soiled paper towels—you know, they have a big metal box with a wedge-shaped cover on top that swings back and forth and you can shove towels in from each side."

Mason nodded. "Find anything, Della?"

"Someone had used the receptacle to dispose of a lot of love letters, and the disposal must either have been very, very, hasty, or else the girl certainly took no precautions to keep anyone who might be interested from getting quite an eyeful. The letters hadn't even been torn through."

"Let's take a look at them," Mason said.

Della Street said, "They were all in one bunch, and I

salvaged the whole outfit. Gosh, I'm glad the rush hour is over. I would have felt pretty self-conscious if someone had come in and caught me digging down in that used towel container!"

Mason's nod showed that he was preoccupied as he examined the letters.

"What do you make of them?" Della Street asked.

"Well," Mason said thoughtfully, "either, as you suggested, the person who left them there was in very much of a hurry, or this was a plant and the person wanted to be certain that the letters would be noticed and could be read without any difficulty. In other words, it's almost too good. A girl trying to dispose of letters would hardly have been so careless about dropping them into the used-towel receptacle in one piece—unless it was a plant of some kind."

"But how about a man?" Della Street asked. "Apparently, the letters were sent to a man and—"

"And they were found in the *ladies'* restroom."

"Yes, that's so."

Mason studied one of the letters. "Now, these are rather peculiar, Della. They are written in a whimsical vein. Listen to this:

"'My dearest Prince Charming,

"'When you rode up on your charger the other night, there were a lot of things I wanted to say to you, but I couldn't think of them until after you had left.

"'Somehow the glittering armor and that formidable helmet made you seem so virtuous and righteous that I felt a distant creature from another and more sordid world. . . . You perhaps don't know it, Prince Charming, but you made quite a handsome spectacle, sitting there with the visor of your helmet raised, your horse with his head down, his flanks heaving and sweating from the exertion of carrying you on that last mission to rescue the damsel in distress, the setting sun reflecting from your polished armor . . .'"

Mason paused, glanced up at Della Street, and said, "What the devil!"

"Take a look at the signature," Della Street said.

Mason turned over two pages and looked at the signature—"Your faithful and devoted Mae."

"You will notice the spelling," Della Street said. "It's M-A-E."

Mason pursed his lips thoughtfully, said, "Now, all we need, Della, is a murder to put us in a thoroughly untenable position."

"What position?"

"That of withholding important evidence from the police."

"You're not going to tell them anything about Mae Wallis?"

Mason shook his head. "I don't dare to, Della. They wouldn't make even the slightest effort to believe me. You can see the position I'd be in. I'd be trying to explain that while the police were making a search of the building in order to find the woman who had broken into the offices of the South African Gem Importing and Exploration Company, I was sitting innocently in my office; that I had no idea that I should have mentioned the typist who dropped in from nowhere at exactly the right time, who seemed completely terrified, who was supposed to have been sent from Miss Mosher's agency, even though, at the time, I *knew* that she hadn't been sent from Miss Mosher's agency."

"Yes," Della Street said, smiling. "With your connections and reputation, I can see that the police would be at least skeptical."

"Very, very skeptical," Mason said. "And since it's bad for the police to develop habits of skepticism, Della, we'll see that they aren't placed in an embarrassing position."

Chapter 4

It was three days later when Perry Mason unlocked the door of his private office and found Della Street waiting for him, his desk carefully cleaned and for once the pile of mail far to one side.

"Chief," Della Street said in a voice of low urgency, "I've been trying to get you. Sit down and let me talk with you before anyone knows you're in."

Mason hung up his hat in the hat closet, seated himself at the desk, glanced at Della Street quizzically and said, "You're certainly worked up. What gives?"

"We have our murder case."

"What do you mean 'our murder case'?"

"Remember what you said about the diamonds? That we only needed a murder case to make the thing perfect?"

Mason came bolt upright in his chair. "What is it, Della? Give me the low-down."

"No one seems to know what it's all about, but Duane Jefferson of the South African Gem Importing and Exploration Company has been arrested for murder. Walter Irving, the other member of the company, is out there in the outer office waiting for you. There's a cablegram from the South African Gem Importing and Exploration Company sent from South Africa, advising you that they are instructing their local representative to pay you two thousand American dollars as a retainer. They want you to represent Duane Jefferson."

"Murder?" Mason said. "Who the devil is the corpse, Della?"

"I don't know. I don't know very much about it. All I know is about the cablegram that came and the fact that

Walter Irving has been in three times to see you. He asked that I notify him just as soon as you arrived, and this last time he decided that he wouldn't even take chances on the delay incident to a telephone call but was going to wait. He wants to see you the minute you come in."

"Send him in, Della. Let's find out what this is all about. Where's that tin box?"

"In the safe."

Mason said, "Where's the desk Mae Wallis was using when she was here?"

"I moved it back into the far corner of the law library."

"Who moved it?"

"I had the janitor and one of his assistants take it in for us."

"How are you on chewing gum, Della?"

"Pretty good. Why?"

Mason said, "Chew some gum, then use it to plaster that wad with the diamonds in it back on the desk in exactly the same place you found it."

"But there'll be a difference in freshness, Chief. That other gum is dry and hard now, and the new gum that I chew will be moist and—"

"And it will dry out if there's a long enough interval," Mason interrupted.

"How long will the interval be?"

"That," Mason told her, "will depend entirely on luck. Send Walter Irving in, Della, and let's see what this is all about."

Della Street nodded and started for the outer office.

"And fix that gum up *right away*," Mason reminded her.

"While Irving is in here?"

Mason nodded.

Della Street went to the outer office and returned with Walter Irving, a well-dressed, heavy-set man who had evidently prepared for the interview by visiting a barber shop. His hair was freshly trimmed, his nails were polished, his face had the smooth pink-and-white appearance which comes from a shave and a massage.

He was about forty-five years old, with reddish-brown, expressionless eyes, and the manner of a man who would show no surprise or emotion if half of the building should suddenly cave in.

"Good morning, Mr. Mason. I guess you don't know me. I've seen you in the elevator and you've been pointed out to me as being the smartest criminal lawyer in the state."

"Thank you," Mason said, shaking hands, and then added dryly, " 'Criminal lawyer' is a popular expression. I prefer to regard myself as a 'trial lawyer.' "

"Well, that's fine," Irving said. "You received a cablegram from my company in South Africa, didn't you?"

"That's right."

"They've authorized me to pay you a retainer for representing my associate, Duane Jefferson."

"That cablegram is a complete mystery to me," Mason said. "What's it all about?"

"I'll come to that in a moment," Irving told him. "I want to get first things first."

"What do you mean?"

"Your fees."

"What about them?"

Irving raised steady eyes to Mason. "Things are different in South Africa."

"Just what are you getting at?"

"Just this," Irving said. "I'm here to protect the interests of my employers, the South African Gem Importing and Exploration Company. It's a big, wealthy company. They want me to turn over a two-thousand-dollar retainer to you. They'd leave it to your discretion as to the balance of the fee. I won't do business that way. On this side of the water, criminal attorneys are inclined to grab all they can get. They— Oh, hell, Mr. Mason, what's the use of beating around the bush? My company has an idea that it's dealing with a barrister in a wig and gown. It doesn't have the faintest idea of how to deal with a criminal lawyer."

"Do you?" Mason asked.

"If I don't I'm sure as hell going to try and find out. I'm protecting my company. How much is it going to cost?"

"You mean the total fee?"

"The total fee."

Mason said, "Tell me about the case, just the general facts and I'll answer your question."

"The facts are utterly cockeyed. Police raided our office. Why, I don't know. They found some diamonds. Those diamonds had been planted. Neither Jefferson nor I had ever seen them before. Our company is just opening up its office here. Some people don't like that."

"What were the diamonds worth?"

"Something like a hundred thousand dollars retail."

"How does murder enter into it?"

"That I don't know."

"Don't you even know who was murdered?"

"A man named Baxter. He's a smuggler."

"Were these his diamonds—the ones the police found in your office?"

"How the hell would *I* know?"

Mason regarded the man for a few seconds, then said, "How the hell would *I* know?"

Irving grinned. "I'm a little touchy this morning."

"So am I. Suppose you start talking."

"All I can tell you for sure is that there's some kind of a frame-up involved. Jefferson never killed anyone. I've known him for years. My gosh, Mr. Mason, look at it this way. Here's a large, exceedingly reputable, ultraconservative company in South Africa. This company has known Duane Jefferson for years. As soon as they hear that he's been arrested, they're willing to put up whatever amount is required in order to secure the very best available representation.

"Mind you, they don't suggest they'll advance Jefferson money to retain counsel. The company itself instructed me to retain the best available counsel for Jefferson."

"And you suggested me?" Mason asked.

"No. I would have, but somebody beat me to it. I got a

cablegram authorizing me to draw a check on our local account in an amount of two thousand dollars and turn that money over to you so you could start taking the necessary legal steps immediately. Now if my company pays your fees, who will your client be?"

"Duane Jefferson."

"Suppose Jefferson tries to get you to do something that isn't in his best interests. What would you do—follow his instructions, or do what was best for him?"

"Why do you ask that question?"

"Duane is trying to protect some woman. He'd let himself get convicted before he'd expose her. He thinks she's wonderful. *I* think she's a clever, two-timing schemer who is out to frame him."

"Who is she?"

"I wish I knew. If I did, I'd have detectives on her trail within the next hour. The trouble is I don't know. I only know there *is* such a woman. She lost her head over Duane. He'll protect her."

"Married?"

"I don't think so. I don't know."

"What about the murder case?"

"It ties in with smuggling. Duane Jefferson sold a batch of diamonds to Munroe Baxter. That was through the South African office. Baxter asked Jefferson to arrange to have the diamonds cut, polished and delivered to our Paris office. Our Paris office didn't know the history of the transaction. It simply made delivery to Baxter on instructions of the South African office. Usually we try to know something about the people with whom we are dealing. Baxter juggled the deal between our two offices in such a way that each office thought the other one had done the investigating.

"Baxter had worked out one hell of a slick scheme. He had faked a perfect background of respectability."

"How did you find out about the smuggling?" Mason asked.

"His female accomplice broke down and confessed."

"Who is she?"

"A girl named Yvonne Manco."

"Tell me about it," Mason said.

"Didn't you read the account about a fellow jumping overboard from a cruise ship and committing suicide a while back?"

"Yes, I did," Mason said. "Wasn't *that* man's name Munroe Baxter?"

"Exactly."

"I knew I'd heard the name somewhere as soon as you mentioned it. How does the murder angle enter into it?"

Irving said, "Here's the general sketch. Yvonne Manco is a very beautiful young woman who sailed on a cruise ship around the world. She was the queen of the cruise. The ship touched at Naples, and when Yvonne started down the gangplank, she was met by Munroe Baxter, a man who had the appearance of a Frenchman, but the name, citizenship and passport of a United States citizen. You must understand all of these things fully in order to appreciate the sequence of events."

"Go ahead," Mason said.

"Apparently, Munroe Baxter had at one time been in love with Yvonne Manco. According to the story that was given to the passengers, they had been going together and then the affair had broken up through a misunderstanding.

"Whoever wrote the script did a beautiful job, Mr. Mason."

"It was a script?" Mason asked.

"Hell, yes. It was as phony as a three dollar bill."

"What happened?"

"The passengers naturally were interested. They saw this man burst through the crowd. They saw him embrace Yvonne Manco. They saw her faint in her arms. There was a beautiful romance, the spice of scandal, a page out of this beautiful young woman's past. It was touching; it was pathetic—and, naturally, it caused an enormous amount of gossip."

Mason nodded.

"The ship was in Naples for two days. It sailed, and

when it sailed Munroe Baxter was pleading with Yvonne Manco to marry him. He was the last man off the ship; then he stood on the pier and wept copiously, shedding crocodile tears."

"Go on," Mason said, interested.

"The ship sailed out into the Mediterranean. It stopped in Genoa. Munroe Baxter met the ship at the dock. Again Yvonne Manco swooned in his arms, again she refused to marry him, again the ship sailed.

"Then came the pay-off. As the ship was off Gibraltar a helicopter hovered overhead. A man descended a rope ladder, dangled precariously from the last rung. The helicopter hovered over the deck of the ship, and Munroe Baxter dropped to the deck by the swimming pool, where Yvonne Manco was disporting herself in the sunlight in a seductive bathing suit."

"Romantic," Mason said.

"And opportune," Irving said dryly. "No one could resist such an impetuous, dramatic courtship. The passengers virtually forced Yvonne to give her consent. The captain married them on the high seas that night. The passengers turned the ship upside down in celebration. It was wonderful stuff."

"Yes, I can imagine," Mason said.

"And, of course," Irving went on, "since Baxter boarded the ship in that dramatic manner, without so much as a toothbrush or an extra handkerchief, how would the customs people suspect that Munroe Baxter was smuggling three hundred thousand dollars' worth of diamonds in a chamois-skin belt around his waist?

"In the face of all that beautiful romance, who would have thought that Yvonne Manco had been Munroe Baxter's mistress for a couple of years, that she was his accomplice in a smuggling plot and that this courtship was all a dramatic hoax?"

"I see," Mason said.

Irving went on, "The stage was all set. Munroe Baxter, in the eyes of the passengers, was a crazy Frenchman, a

United States citizen, of course, but one who had acquired all the excitability of the French.

"So, when the ship approached port and Yvonne Manco, dressed to the hilt, danced three times with the good-looking assistant purser, it was only natural that Munroe Baxter should stage a violent scene, threaten to kill himself, break into tears, dash to his stateroom and subsequently leap overboard after a frenzied scene in which Yvonne Manco threatened to divorce him."

"Yes," Mason said, "I remember the newspapers made quite a play of the story."

"It was made to order for press coverage," Irving said. "And who would have thought that the excitable Munroe Baxter carried with him three hundred thousand dollars in diamonds when he jumped overboard, that he was a powerful swimmer who could easily swim to a launch which was opportunely waiting at a pre-arranged spot, and that later on he and the lovely Yvonne were to share the proceeds of a carefully written, superbly directed scenario, performed very cleverly for the sole purpose of fooling the customs men?"

"And it didn't?" Mason asked.

"Oh, but it did! Everything went like clockwork, except for one thing—Munroe Baxter didn't reappear to join Yvonne Manco. She went to the secluded motel which was to be their rendezvous. She waited and waited and waited and waited."

"Perhaps Baxter decided that a whole loaf was better than half a loaf," Mason said.

Irving shook his head. "It seems the lovely Yvonne Manco went to the accomplice who was waiting in the launch. At first, the accomplice told her that Baxter had never showed up. He told her that Baxter must have been seized by cramps while he was swimming underwater."

"Did this take place within the territorial waters of the United States?" Mason asked.

"Right at the approach to Los Angeles Harbor."

"In daylight?"

"No, just before daylight. You see, it was a cruise ship and it was gliding in at the earliest possible hour so the passengers could have a maximum time ashore for sight-seeing."

"All right, Baxter was supposed to have drowned," Mason said. "What happened?"

"Well, Yvonne Manco had a horrible suspicion. She thought that the accomplice in the launch might have held Baxter's head underwater and might have taken the money belt.

"Probably, she wouldn't have said anything at all, if it hadn't been for the fact that customs agents were also putting two and two together. They called on the lovely Yvonne Manco to question her about her 'husband' after it appeared that she and her 'husband' had sailed on another cruise ship as man and wife some eighteen months earlier."

"And Yvonne Manco broke down and told them the whole story?" Mason asked.

"Told them the whole story, including the part that it had been Duane Jefferson who had been involved in the sale of the jewels. So police became very much interested in Duane Jefferson, and yesterday afternoon, on an affidavit of Yvonne Manco, a search warrant was issued and police searched the office."

"And recovered a hundred thousand dollars in gems?" Mason asked.

"Recovered a goodly assortment of diamonds," Irving said. "Let us say, perhaps a third of the value of the smuggled shipment."

"And the remaining two-thirds?"

Irving shrugged his shoulders.

"And the identification?" Mason asked.

Again Irving shrugged his shoulders.

"And where were these gems found?"

"Where someone had very cleverly planted them. You may remember the little flurry of excitement when an intruder was discovered in the office—the police asked us to check and see if anything had been taken. It never occurred to us to check *and see if anything had been planted.*"

"Where were the diamonds found?"

"In a package fastened to the back of a desk drawer with adhesive tape."

"And what does Duane Jefferson have to say about this?"

"What could he say?" Irving asked. "It was all news to him, just as it was to me."

"You can vouch for these facts?" Mason asked.

"I'll vouch for them. But I can't vouch for Duane's romantic, crazy notions of protecting this girl."

"She was the same girl who entered the office?"

"I think she was. Duane would have a fit and never speak to me again if he knew I ever entertained such a thought. You have to handle him with kid gloves where women are concerned. But if it comes to a showdown, *you're* going to have to drag this girl into it, and Duane Jefferson will cease to co-operate with you as soon as you mention her very existence."

Mason thought the matter over.

"Well?" Irving asked.

"Make out your check for two thousand dollars," Mason told him. "That will be on account of a five-thousand dollar fee."

"What do you mean—a five-thousand-dollar fee?"

"It won't be more than that."

"Including detectives?"

"No. You will have to pay expenses. I'm fixing fees."

"Damn it," Irving exploded. "If that bunch in the home office hadn't mentioned a two-thousand-dollar retainer, I could have got you to handle the whole case for two thousand."

Mason sat quietly facing Irving.

"Well, it's done now, and there's nothing I can do about it," Irving said, taking from his wallet a check already made out to the lawyer. He slid the check across the desk to Perry Mason.

Mason said to Della Street, "Make a receipt, Della, and put on the receipt that this is a retainer on behalf of Duane Jefferson."

"What's the idea?" Irving asked.

"Simply to show that I'm not responsible to you or your company but only to my client."

Irving thought that over.

"Any objections?" Mason asked.

"No. I presume you're intimating that you'd even turn against me if it suited Duane's interests for you to do so."

"I'm more than intimating. I'm telling you."

Irving grinned. "That's okay by me. I'll go further. If at any time things start getting hot, you can count on me to do anything needed to back your play. I'd even consent to play the part of a missing witness."

Mason shook his head. "Don't try to call the plays. Let me do that."

Irving extended his hand. "I just want you to understand my position, Mason."

"And be sure *you* understand *mine*," Mason said.

Chapter 5

Mason looked at Della Street as Walter Irving left the office.

"Well?" Della Street asked.

Mason said, "I just about had to take the case in self-defense, Della."

"Why?"

"Otherwise, we'd be sitting on top of information in a murder case, we wouldn't have any client whom we would be protecting, and the situation could become rather rugged."

"And as it is now?" she asked.

"Now," he told her, "we have a client whom we can be protecting. An attorney representing a client in a murder case is under no obligation to go to the police and set forth his surmises, suspicions, and conclusions, particularly if he has reason to believe that such a course would be against the best interests of his client."

"But how about the positive evidence?" Della Street asked.

"Evidence of what?"

"Evidence that we harbored a young woman who had gone into that office and planted diamonds."

"We don't *know* she planted diamonds."

"Who had gone into the office then."

"We don't *know* she was the same woman."

"It's a reasonable assumption."

"Suppose she was merely a typist who happened to be in the building. We go to the police with a lot of suspicions, and the police give the story to the newspapers, then she sues for defamation of character."

"I see," Della Street said demurely. "I'm afraid it's hopeless to try and convince you."

"It is."

"And now may I ask you a question, Counselor?"

"What?"

"Do you suppose that it was pure coincidence that you are the attorney retained to represent the interests of Duane Jefferson?"

Mason stroked his chin thoughtfully.

"Well?" she prompted.

"I've thought of that," Mason admitted. "Of course, the fact that I am known as a trial attorney, that I have offices on the same floor of the same building would mean that Irving had had a chance to hear about me and, by the same token, a chance to notify his home office that I would be available."

"But he said he didn't do that. He said somebody beat him to it and he got the cable to turn over the two thousand dollars to you."

Mason nodded.

"Well?" Della Street asked.

"No comment," Mason said.

"So what do we do now?"

"Now," Mason said, "our position is very, very clear, Della. I suggest that you go down to the camera store, tell them that I want to buy a fingerprint camera, and you also might get a studio camera with a ground-glass focusing arrangement. Pick up some lights and we'll see if we can get a photograph of those latent fingerprints on the gum."

"And then?" she asked.

"Then," Mason said, "we'll enlarge the film so that it shows only the fingerprints and not the gum."

"And then?"

"By that time," Mason said, "I hope we have managed to locate the girl who made the fingerprints and find out about things for ourselves. While you're getting the cameras I'll go down to Paul Drake's office and have a chat with him."

"Chief," Della Street asked somewhat apprehensively, "isn't this rather risky?"

Mason's grin was infectious. "Sure it is."

"Hadn't you better forget about other things and protect yourself?"

Mason shook his head. "We're protecting a client, Della. Give me a description of that girl—the best one you can give."

"Well," Della Street said, "I'd place her age at twenty-six or twenty-seven, her height at five feet three inches, her weight at about a hundred and sixteen pounds. She had reddish-brown hair and her eyes were also a reddish-brown—about the same color as her hair, very expressive. She was good-looking, trim and well proportioned."

"Good figure?" Mason asked.

"Perfect."

"How was she dressed?"

"I can remember that quite well, Chief, because she looked stunning. I remember thinking at the time that she looked more like a client than a gal from an employment agency.

"She wore a beautifully tailored gray flannel suit, navy blue kid shoes. Umm, let me see . . . yes, I remember now. There was fine white stitching across the toes of the shoes. She carried a matching envelope purse and white gloves. Now let me think. I am quite sure she didn't wear a hat. As I recall, she had a tortoise-shell band on, and there wasn't a hair out of place.

"She didn't take her jacket off while she was working, so I can't be certain, but I think she had on a pale blue cashmere sweater. She opened just the top button of her jacket, so I can't say for sure about this."

Mason smiled. "You women never miss a thing about another woman, do you, Della? I would say that was remembering *very* well. Would you type it out for me—the description? Use a plain sheet of paper, not my letterhead.'

Mason waited until Della Street had finished typing the description, then said, "Okay, Della, go down and get the cameras. Get lots of film, lights, a tripod, and anything we may need. Don't let on what we want to use them for."

"The fingerprint camera—isn't that a giveaway?"

"Tell the proprietor I'm going to have to cross-examine a witness and I want to find out all about how a fingerprint camera works."

Della Street nodded.

Mason took the typed description and walked down the hall to Paul Drake's office. He nodded to the girl at the switchboard. "Paul Drake in?"

"Yes, Mr. Mason. Shall I say you're here?"

"Anybody with him?"

"No."

"Tell him I'm on my way," Mason said, opening the gate in the partition and walking down the long glassed-in runway off which there were numerous cubbyhole offices. He came to the slightly more commodious office marked "Paul Drake, Private," pushed open the door and entered.

"Hi," Drake said. "I was waiting to hear from you."

Mason raised his eyebrows.

"Don't look so innocent," Drake said. "The officials of the South African Gem Importing and Exploration Company have been checking up on you by long-distance telephone. They called the manager of the building and asked him about you."

"Did they ask him about me by name," Mason asked, "or did they ask him to recommend some attorney?"

"No, they had your name. They wanted to know all about you."

"What did he tell them?"

Drake grinned and said, "Your rent's paid up, isn't it?"

"What the devil is this all about, do you know, Paul?"

"All I know is it's a murder rap," Drake said, "and the way the police are acting, someone must have caved in with a confession."

"Sure," Mason said, "a confession that would pass the buck to someone else and take the heat off the person making the so-called confession."

"Could be," Drake said. "What do we do?"

"We get busy."

"On what?"

"First," Mason told him, "I want to find a girl."

"Okay, what do I have to go on?"

Mason handed him Della Street's typewritten description.

"Fine," Drake said. "I can go downstairs, stand on the street corner during the lunch hour and pick you out a hundred girls of this description in ten minutes."

"Take another look," Mason invited. "She's a lot better than average."

"If it was average, I could make it a thousand," Drake said.

"All right," Mason said. "We're going to have to narrow it down."

"How?"

"This girl," Mason said, "is an expert typist. She probably holds down a very good secretarial job somewhere."

"Unless, of course, she *was* an exceedingly fine secretary and then got married," Drake said.

Mason nodded, conceding the point without changing his position. "She also has legal experience," he said.

"How do you know?"

"That's something I'm not at liberty to tell you."

"All right, what do I do?"

Mason said, "Paul you're going to have to open up a dummy office. You're going to telephone the Association of Legal Secretaries; you're going to put an ad in the bar journal and the newspapers; you're going to ask for a young, attractive typist. Now, I don't *know* that this girl takes shorthand. Therefore, you're going to have to state that a knowledge of shorthand is desirable but not necessary. You're going to offer a salary of two hundred dollars a week—"

"My Lord!" Drake said. "You'll be deluged, Perry. You might just as well ask the whole city to come trooping into your office."

"Wait a minute," Mason told him. "You don't have the sketch yet."

"Well, I certainly hope I don't!"

"Your ad will provide that the girl must pass a typing test in order to get the job. She must be able to copy rapidly and perfectly and at a very high rate of speed—fix a top rate of words per minute.

"Now, the type of girl we want will already have a job somewhere. We've got to get a job that sounds sufficiently attractive so she'll come in to take a look. Therefore, we can't expect her in during office hours. So mention that the office will be open noons and until seven o'clock in the evening."

"And you want me to rent a furnished office?" Drake asked.

"That's right."

Drake said lugubriously, "You'd better make arrangements to replace the carpet when you leave. The one that's there will be worn threadbare by the horde of applicants— How the devil will I know if the right girl comes in?"

"That's what I'm coming to," Mason said. "You're going to start looking these applicants over. You won't find many that can type at the rate specified. Be absolutely hardboiled with the qualifications. Have a good secretary sitting there, weeding them out. Don't pay any attention to anyone who has to reach for an eraser. The girl I want can make that keyboard sound like a machine gun."

"Okay, then what?"

"When you get girls who qualify on the typing end of the job," Mason said, "give them a personal interview. Look them over carefully to see how they check with this description and tell them you want to see their driving licenses. A girl like that is bound to have a car. That's where the catch comes in."

"How come?"

Mason said, "Sometime this afternoon I'm going to send you over a right thumbprint—that is, a photograph of a thumbprint—perhaps not the best fingerprinting in the world but at least you'll be able to identify it. When you look at their driving licenses, make it a point to be called into another room for something. Get up and excuse yourself. You can say that there's another applicant in there that you have to talk to briefly, or that you have to answer a phone or something. Carry the girl's driving license in there with you, give the thumbprint a quick check. You can eliminate most of them at a glance. Some of them you may have to study a little bit. But if you get the right one, you'll be able to recognize the thumbprint pretty quickly."

"What do I do then?"

"Make a note of the name and address on the driving license. In that way, she won't be able to give you a phony name. And call me at once."

"Anything else?" Drake asked.

"This is what I think," Mason said, "but it's just a hunch. I *think* the girl's first name will be Mae. When you find a girl who answers that general description and can type like a house afire, whose first name is Mae, start checking carefully."

"When will you have that thumbprint?"

"Sometime this afternoon. Her driving license will have the imprint of her right thumb on it."

"Can you tell me what this is all about?" Drake asked.

Mason grinned and shook his head. "It's better if you don't know, Paul."

"One of those things, eh?" Drake asked, his voice showing a singular lack of enthusiasm.

"No," Mason told him, "it isn't. It's just that I'm taking an ounce of prevention."

"With you," Drake told him, "I prefer a *pound* of prevention. If things go wrong, I know there won't be more than an ounce of cure."

Chapter 6

Mason sat in the visitors' room at the jail and looked across at Duane Jefferson.

His client was a tall, composed individual who seemed reserved, unexcited, and somehow very British.

Mason tried to jar the man out of his extraordinary complacency.

"You're charged with murder," he said.

Duane Jefferson observed him coolly. "I would hardly be here otherwise, would I?"

"What do you know about this thing?"

"Virtually nothing. I knew the man, Baxter, in his lifetime—that is, I assume it was the same one."

"How did you know him?"

"He represented himself as a big wholesale dealer. He showed up at the South African office and wanted to buy diamonds. It is against the policy of the company to sell diamonds in the rough, unless, of course, they are industrial diamonds."

"Baxter wanted them in the rough?"

"That's right."

"And he was advised he couldn't have them?"

"Well, of course, we were tactful about it, Mr. Mason. Mr. Baxter gave promise of being an excellent customer, and he was dealing on a cash basis."

"So what was done?"

"We showed him some diamonds that were cut and polished. He didn't want those. He said that the deal he was putting across called for buying diamonds in the rough and carrying them through each step of cutting and polishing. He said he wanted to be able to tell his customers he had personally selected the diamonds just as they came from the fields."

"Why?"

"He didn't say."

"And he wasn't asked?"

"In a British-managed company," Jefferson said, "we try to keep personal questions to a minimum. We don't pry, Mr. Mason."

"So what was done finally?"

"It was arranged that he would select the diamonds, that we would send them to our Paris office, that there they would be cut and polished, and, after they were cut and polished, delivery would be made to Mr. Baxter."

"What were the diamonds worth?"

"Wholesale or retail?"

"Wholesale."

"Very much less than their retail price."

"How much less?"

"I can't tell you."

"Why not?"

"That information is a very closely guarded trade secret, Mr. Mason."

"But I'm your attorney."

"Quite."

"Look here," Mason said, "are you British?"

"No."

"American?"

"Yes."

"How long have you been working for a British company?"

"Five or six years."

"You have become quite British."

"There are certain mannerisms, Mr. Mason, which the trade comes to expect of the representatives of a company such as ours."

"And there are certain mannerisms which an American jury expects to find in an American citizen," Mason told him.

"If a jury should feel you'd cultivated a British manner, you might have reason to regret your accent and cool, impersonal detachment."

Jefferson's lip seemed to curl slightly. "I would have nothing but contempt for a jury that would let personal considerations such as those influence its judgment."

"That would break the jurors' hearts," Mason told him.

Jefferson said, "We may as well understand each other at the outset, Mr. Mason. I govern my actions according to principle. I would rather die than yield in a matter of principle."

"All right," Mason said. "Have it your own way. It's your funeral. Did you see Baxter again?"

"No, sir, I didn't. After that, arrangements were completed through the Paris office."

"Irving?" Mason asked.

"I don't think it was Irving, Mr. Mason. I think it was one of the other representatives."

"You read about the arrival of the cruise ship and Baxter's supposed suicide?"

"I did, indeed, Mr. Mason."

"And did you make any comment to the authorities?"

"Certainly not."

"You knew he was carrying a small fortune in diamonds?"

"I assumed that a small fortune in diamonds had been delivered to him through our Paris office. I had no means, of course, of knowing what he had done with them."

"You didn't make any suggestions to the authorities?"

"Certainly not. Our business dealings are highly confidential."

"But you did discuss his death with your partner, Irving?"

"Not a partner, Mr. Mason. A representative of the company, a personal friend but—"

"All right, your associate," Mason corrected.

"Yes, I discussed it with him."

"Did he have any ideas?"

"None. Except that there were certain suspicious circumstances in connection with the entire situation."

"It occurred to you that the whole thing might have been part of a smuggling plot?"

"I prefer not to amplify that statement, Mr. Mason. I can simply say that there were certain suspicious circumstances in connection with the entire transaction."

"And you discussed those with Irving?"

"As a representative of the company talking to an associate, I did. I would prefer, however, not to go into detail as to what I said. You must remember, Mr. Mason, that I am here not in an individual but a representative capacity."

"You may be in this country in a representative capacity," Mason said, "but don't ever forget that you're here in this jail in a purely individual capacity."

"Oh, quite," Jefferson said.

"I understand police found diamonds in your office," Mason went on.

Jefferson nodded.

"Where did those diamonds come from?"

"Mr. Mason, I haven't the faintest idea. I am in my office approximately six hours out of the twenty-four. I believe the building provides a scrubwoman with a master key. The janitor also has a master key. People come and go through that office. Police even told me that there was someone trying to break into the office, or that someone had broken into the office."

"A girl," Mason said.

"I understand it was a young woman, yes."

"Do you have any idea who this woman was?"

"No. Certainly not!"

"Do you know any young women here in the city?"

Jefferson hesitated.

"Do you?" Mason prodded.

Jefferson met his eyes. "No."

"You're acquainted with *no* young woman?"

"No."

"Would you perhaps be trying to shield someone?"

"Why should I try to shield someone?"

"I am not asking you why at the moment. I am asking you if you are."

"No."

"You understand it could be a very serious matter if you should try to falsify any of the facts?"

"Isn't it a rule of law in this country," Jefferson countered, "that the prosecution must prove the defendant guilty beyond all reasonable doubt?"

Mason nodded.

"They can't do it," Jefferson said confidently.

"You may not have another chance to tell me your story," Mason warned.

"I've told it."

"There is no girl?"

"No."

"Weren't you writing to some young woman here before you left South Africa?"

Again there was a perceptible hesitancy, then Jefferson looked him in the eyes and said, "No."

"Police told you there was some young woman who broke into your office?"

"Someone who opened the door with a key."

"Had you given your key to any woman?"

"No. Certainly not."

Mason said, "Look here, if there's anyone you want protected, tell me the whole story. I'll try to protect that person as far as possible. After all, I'm representing you. I'm trying to do what is for your best interests. Now, don't put yourself in such a position that you're going to have to try to deceive your attorney. Do you understand what that can lead to?"

"I understand."

"And you are protecting no one?"

"No one."

"The district attorney's office feels that it has some

evidence against you, otherwise it wouldn't be proceeding in a case of this kind."

"I suppose a district attorney can be mistaken as well as anyone else."

"Better sometimes," Mason said. "You're not being very helpful."

"What help can I give, Mr. Mason? Suppose *you* should walk into your office tomorrow morning and find the police there. Suppose they told you that they had uncovered stolen property in your office. Suppose I should ask you to tell me the entire story. What could you tell me?"

"I'd try to answer your questions."

"I have answered your questions, Mr. Mason."

"I have reason to believe there's some young woman here in the city whom you know."

"There is no one."

Mason got to his feet. "Well," he told the young man, "it's up to you."

"On the contrary, Mr. Mason. I think you'll find that it's up to *you*."

"You're probably right, at that," Mason told him, and signaled the guard that the interview was over.

Chapter 7

Mason unlocked the door of his private office. Della Street looked up from her work. "How did it go, Chief?"

Mason made a gesture of throwing something away.

"Not talking?" Della Street asked.

"Talking," Mason said, "but it doesn't make sense. He's protecting some woman."

"Why?"

"That," Mason said, "is something we're going to have to find out. Get the cameras, Della?"

"Yes. Cameras, lights, films, tripod—everything."

"We're going into the photographic business," Mason said. "Tell Gertie we don't want to be disturbed, no matter what happens."

Della Street started to pick up the connecting telephone to the outer office, then hesitated. "Gertie is going to make something out of *this!*" she said.

Mason frowned thoughtfully. "You have a point there," he said.

"With her romantic disposition, she will get ideas in her head that you'll never get out with a club."

"All right," Mason decided. "Don't let her know I'm in. We'll just go into the law library and—do you think you could help me tilt that desk over on its side, Della?"

"I can try."

"Good. We'll just go into the library, close and lock the door."

"Suppose Gertie should want me for something? Can't we tell her what we're doing so she can—"

Mason shook his head. "I don't want *anyone* to know about this, Della."

Della went through the motions of throwing something in the wastebasket. "There goes my good name," she said.

"You'll need to stay only to help me get the desk over on its side, and you can fix up the lighting. We'll lock the door from the law library to the outer office and leave the door to this office open. You can hear the phone if Gertie rings."

"That's all right," Della Street said, "but suppose she comes in for something?"

"Well, if the door's open," Mason said, "she'll see that we're photographing something."

"Her curiosity is as bad as her romanticism," Della said.

"Does she talk?" Mason asked.

"I wish I knew the answer to that one, Chief. She must talk to that boy friend of hers. You couldn't keep Gertie quiet with a muzzle. I doubt that she talks to anyone else."

"Okay," Mason said, "we'll take a chance. Come on, Della. Let's get that desk on its side and get the floodlights rigged up."

"Here's a chart," Della Street said, "giving all the exposure factors. I told the man at the camera store we wanted to copy some documents. You have to change your exposure factor when you do real close-up photography. He suggested that we use film packs with the camera where you focus on the ground glass. The fingerprint camera is supposed to be a self-contained unit, with lights and every—"

"I understand," Mason interrupted. "I want to get the wad of chewing gum photographed in place on the bottom of the desk, then I want to get close-ups showing the fingerprints. We can get the photographer to enlarge the fingerprints from these photographs in case the fingerprint camera doesn't do a good job."

"The fingerprint camera seems to be pretty near—" She paused suddenly.

Mason laughed. "Foolproof?"

"Well," Della Street said, "that's what the man at the camera store said."

"All right," Mason told her, "let's go. We'll take

photographs at different exposures. You have plenty of film packs?"

"Heavens, yes! I figured you'd want to be sure you had the job done, and I got enough film so you can take all the pictures you want at all kinds of different exposures."

"That's fine," Mason told her.

Della Street took one end of the typewriter desk, Mason the other. "We'll have to move it out from the wall," Mason said. "Now tilt it back, Della. It'll be heavy just before it gets to the floor. You think you can—?"

"Good heavens, yes, Chief. It's not heavy."

"The drawers are full of stationery, and that typewriter— We could take some of the things out and lighten it."

"No, no, let's go. It's all right."

They eased the desk back to the floor.

"All right," Mason said, "give me a hand with the lights and the tripod. We'll get this camera set up and focused."

"I have a magnifying glass," Della Street said. "They seem to think that on the critical focusing necessary for close-ups it will help."

"Good girl," Mason told her. "Let's see what we can do. We'll want an unbalanced cross-lighting, and since light varies inversely as the square of the distance, we'll space these lights accordingly."

Mason first took a series of pictures with the fingerprint camera, then got the lights plugged in and adjusted, the studio camera placed on the tripod and properly focused. He used a tape measure to determine the position of the lights, then slipped a film pack into the camera, regarded the wad of chewing gum thoughtfully.

"That's going to be fine," Della Street said. "How did you know about using unbalanced cross-lighting to bring out the ridges?"

"Cross-examining photographers," Mason said, "plus a study of books on photography. A lawyer has to know a little something about everything. Don't you notice *Photographic Evidence* by Scott over there?" Mason indicated the book bound in red leather.

54

"That's right," she said. "I remember seeing you studying that from time to time. You used some of his stuff in that automobile case, didn't you?"

"Uh huh," Mason said. "It's surprising how much there is to know about photography. Now, Della, I'm going to start with this lens at $f11$, taking a photograph at a twenty-fifth of a second. Then we'll take one at a tenth of a second, then one at a second. Then I'll use the cable release and we'll take one at two seconds. Then we'll try $f16$, run through the exposures all over again, then take another batch at $f22$."

"All right," Della Street said. "I'll keep notes of the different exposures."

Mason started taking the pictures, pulling the tabs out of the film pack, tearing them off, dropping them into the wastebasket.

"Oh oh," Della Street said. "There's the phone. That's Gertie calling."

She made a dash for Mason's private office. Mason continued taking pictures.

Della Street was back after a moment. "Walter Irving wants you to call just as soon as you come in."

Mason nodded.

"Gertie asked if you were in yet, and I lied like a trooper," Della Street said.

"Okay, Della. Walter Irving didn't say what he wanted, did he?"

"He said he wanted to know if you'd been able to get any information out of Duane Jefferson about the woman in the case."

Mason said, "As soon as we get finished here, Della, tell Paul Drake I want to put a shadow on Irving."

"You suspect him?"

"Not exactly. The policy of this office is to protect our client and to hell with the rest of them."

"What's the client doing?"

"Sitting tight. Says he knows nothing about the girl who

broke into the office, that he doesn't know any girl here, hasn't been corresponding with anyone, and all that."

"You think he has?"

"That wasn't just a casual visit that Mae Wallis paid to their office."

"You've decided she was the girl?"

"Oh, not officially. I'd deny it to the police. But where did the diamonds in the chewing gum come from?"

"Chief, why would *she* plant a hundred thousand dollars' worth of diamonds and then keep a couple of diamonds with her and conceal them in a wad of chewing gum?"

"I can give you *an* answer," Mason said, "but it may not be *the* answer."

"What is it?"

"Suppose she had been given some gems to plant. She must have had them wrapped in tissue paper in her purse. She had to work in a hurry and probably became somewhat alarmed. Something happened to make her suspicious. She realized that she had been detected."

"What makes you say that?"

"Because she roughed up the office, making it appear she was looking *for* something. Otherwise she'd have slipped in, planted the diamonds and left."

"Then you think the diamonds that she put in the chewing gum were ones she had overlooked when she was making the plant?"

"I said it was *an* answer. After she got established as a typist in our office, she had a breathing spell. She opened her purse to make sure she hadn't overlooked anything, and found several of the diamonds. She knew that police were on the job and that there was a good chance she might be picked up, questioned, and perhaps searched. So she fastened the diamonds to the underside of the desk."

"I keep thinking those 'Prince Charming' letters have something to do with it, Chief."

Mason nodded. "So do I. Perhaps she planted the diamonds in the office and at the same time deliberately planted the letters in the restroom."

"She could have done that, all right," Della Street admitted. "There's the phone again."

She gathered her skirts and again sprinted for Mason's private office. Mason continued to take photographs while she answered the phone and returned.

"What is it?" Mason asked.

"I have to announce," she said, "that Gertie is just a little suspicious."

"Yes?" Mason asked.

"Yes. She wants to know why it's taking me so long to answer the phone."

"What did you tell her?"

"Told her I was doing some copy work and I didn't want to stop in the middle of a sentence."

Mason snapped out the floodlights. "All right, Della. We'll quit. We have enough pictures. Tell Paul Drake I want shadows put on Walter Irving."

Chapter 8

A few mornings later Mason was scanning the papers on his desk. "Well, I see that the grand jury has now filed an indictment, charging Duane Jefferson with first-degree murder."

"Why the indictment?" Della Street asked.

"The district attorney can proceed against a defendent in either of two ways. He can file a complaint or have someone swear to a complaint. Then the Court holds a preliminary hearing. At that time the defendant can cross-examine the witnesses. If the Court makes an order binding the defendant over, the district attorney then files an information and the case is brought on to trial before a jury.

"However, the district attorney can, if he wishes, present witnesses to the grand jury. The grand jury then returns an indictment, and the transcript of the testimony of the witnesses is delivered to the defendant. In that case, there is no opportunity for counsel for the defense to cross-examine the witnesses until they get to court.

"Now, in this case against Duane Jefferson, the main witness before the grand jury seems to have been Yvonne Manco, who tells a great story about how her lover-boy, Munroe Baxter, was rubbed out by some nasty people who wanted to steal the diamonds he was smuggling. Then there is the testimony of a police officer that a large portion of those diamonds was found in the office occupied by Duane Jefferson."

"Is that testimony sufficient to support an indictment?" Della Street asked.

Mason grinned and said, "It certainly wouldn't be

sufficient standing by itself to bring about a conviction in a court of law."

"Do you intend to question the sufficiency of the evidence?"

"Lord, no," Mason said. "For some reason the district attorney is breaking his neck to get a prompt trial, and I'm going to co-operate by every means in my power."

"Wouldn't it be better to stall the thing along a bit until—?"

Mason shook his head.

"Why not, Chief?"

"Well, the rumor is that the district attorney has a surprise witness he's going to throw at us. He's so intent on that he may overlook the fact that there isn't any real *corpus delicti*."

"What do you mean?"

"The body of Munroe Baxter has never been found," Mason said.

"Does it have to be?"

"Not necessarily. The words *corpus dilecti*, contrary to popular belief, don't mean the 'body of the victim.' They mean the 'body of the crime.' But it *is* necessary to show that a murder was committed. That can be shown by independent evidence, but of course the *best* evidence is the body of the victim."

"So you're going to have an immediate trial?"

"Just as soon as we can get an open date on the calendar," Mason said. "And with the district attorney and the defense both trying to get the earliest possible trial date, that shouldn't be too difficult. How's Paul Drake coming with his office setup?"

"Chief, you should see that. It's wonderful! There's this ad in all of the papers, advertising for a legally trained secretary who can type like a house afire. The salary to start—to start, mind you—is two hundred dollars a week. It is intimated that the attorney is engaged in cases of international importance and that there may be an opportunity to travel, to meet important personalities. It's a secretary's dream."

"And the office where he's screening applicants?" Mason asked.

"All fitted out with desks, typewriters, law books, plush carpets and an air of quiet dignity which makes it seem that even the janitor must be drawing a salary about equal to that of the ordinary corporation president."

"I hope he hasn't overdone it," Mason said. "I'd better take a look."

"No, it isn't overdone. I can assure you of that. The air of conservatism and respectibility envelops the place like a curtain of smog, permeating every nook and cranny of the office. You should see them—stenographers who are applicants come in chewing gum, giggling and willing to take a chance that lightning may strike despite their lack of qualifications. They stand for a few seconds in that office, then quietly remove their gum, look around at the furniture and start talking in whispers."

"How does he weed out the incompetents?" Mason asked.

"There's a battery of typewriters; girls are asked to sit at the typewriters, write out their names and addresses and list their qualifications.

"Of course, a good typist can tell the minute a girl's hands touch the keyboard whether she is really skillful, fairly competent, or just mediocre. Only the girls who can really play a tune on the keyboard get past the first receptionist."

"Well," Mason said, "it's—"

The private, unlisted phone jangled sharply.

"Good Lord," Della Street said, "that must be Paul now. He's the only other one who has that number."

Mason grabbed for the phone. "That means he's got imformation so hot he doesn't dare to go through the outer switchboard. Hello . . . hello, Paul."

Drake's voice came over the wire. He was talking rapidly

but in the hushed tones of one who is trying to keep his voice from being heard in an adjoining room.

"Hello, Perry. Hello, Perry. This is Paul."

"Yes, Paul, go ahead."

"I have your girl."

"You're certain?"

"Yes."

"Who is she?"

"Her name is Mae W. Jordan. She lives at Seven-Nine-Two Cabachon Street. She's employed at the present time in a law office. She doesn't want to give the name. She would have to give two weeks' notice. She wants the job very badly, and, boy, can that girl tickle the typewriter! And it's wonderful typing."

"What does the *W* stand for?" Mason asked. "Wallis?"

"I don't know yet. I'm just giving you a quick flash that we have the girl."

"You know it's the same one?"

"Yes. The thumbprints match. I'm holding her driving license right at the moment."

"How about the address?" Mason asked.

"And the address is okay. It's Seven-Nine-Two Cabachon Street, the same address that's given on her driving license."

"Okay," Mason said. "Now here's what you do, Paul. Tell her that you *think* she can do the job; that you'll have to arrange an appointment with Mr. Big himself for six o'clock tonight. Tell her to return then. Got that?"

"I've got it," Drake said. "Shall I tell her anything else about the job?"

"No," Mason said. "Try and find out what you can. Be interested but not *too* curious."

"You want me to put a shadow on her?"

"Not if you're certain of the address," Mason said.

"Think we should try to find out about the law office where she's working?"

"No," Mason said. "With her name and address we can get everything we need. This girl is smart and sharp, and

61

she may be mixed up in a murder, Paul. She's undoubtedly connected in some way with a diamond-smuggling operation. Too many questions will—"

"I get it," Drake interrupted. "Okay, Perry, I'll fix an appointment for six o'clock and call you back in fifteen or twenty minutes."

"Do better than that," Mason said. "As soon as you've finished with this girl, jump in your car and come up here. There's no use waiting around there any longer. We've found what we were looking for. You can close the office tomorrow. Take your ads out of the papers and tell all other applicants that the job has been filled. Let's start cutting down the expense."

"Okay," Drake said.

Mason hung up the phone and grinned at Della Street. "Well, we have our typist, Della. She's Mae W. Jordan of Seven-Nine-Two Cabachon Street. Make a note of that— and keep the note where no one else can find it."

Chapter 9

Paul Drake was grinning with the satisfaction of a job well done as he eased himself into the big overstuffed chair in Perry Mason's office.

"Well, we did it, Perry, but it certainly was starting from scratch and working on slender clues."

Mason flashed Della Street a glance. "It was a nice job, Paul."

"What gave you your lead in the first place?" Drake asked.

"Oh," Mason said with a gesture of dismissal, "it was just a hunch."

"But you had a damn good thumbprint," Drake said.

"Purely fortuitous," Mason observed.

"Well, if you don't want to tell me, I don't suppose you will," Drake said. "I see they've indicted Jefferson."

"That's right."

"The district attorney says there are certain factors in the situation which demand a speedy trial in order to keep evidence from being dissipated."

"Uh huh," Mason said noncommittally.

"You going to stall around and try for delay?"

"Why should I?"

"Well, ordinarily when the D.A. wants something, the attorney for the defense has different ideas."

"This isn't an ordinary case, Paul."

"No, I suppose not."

"What have you found out about Irving?" Mason asked.

Drake pulled a notebook from his pocket. "Full name, Walter Stockton Irving. Been with the Paris branch of the South African Gem Importing and Exploration Company for about seven years. Likes life on the Continent, the broader standards of morality, the more leisurely pace of life. Quite a race horse fan."

"The deuce he is!"

"That's right. Of course, over there it isn't quite the way it is here."

"A gambler?"

"Well, not exactly. He'll get down to Monte Carlo once in a while and do a little plunging, but mostly he likes to get out with a pair of binoculars and a babe on his arm, swinging a cane, enjoying the prerogatives of being a quote gentleman unquote."

"Now that," Mason said, "interests me a lot, Paul."

"I thought it would."

"What's he doing with his time here?"

"Simply waiting for the branch to get ready for business. He's leading a subdued life. Doubtless the murder charge pending against Jefferson is holding him back slightly. He seems to have made one contact."

"Who?" Mason asked.

"A French babe. Marline Chaumont."

"Where?"

"A bungalow out on Ponce de Leon Drive. The number is 8257."

"Does Marline Chaumont live there alone?"

"No. She has a brother she's taking care of."

"What's wrong with the brother?"

"Apparently he's a mental case. He was released from a hospital, so that his sister could take care of him. However, elaborate precautions are being taken to keep the neighbors from knowing anything about it. One of the neighbors suspects, but that's as far as it goes at the present time."

"Violent?" Mason asked.

"No, not at this time. Just harmless. You've heard of prefrontal lobotomy?"

"Yes, sure. That's the treatment they formerly used on the hopelessly violent insane and on criminals. I understand they've more or less discontinued it."

"Turns a man into a vegetable more or less, doesn't it?"

"Well, you can't get doctors to agree on it," Mason said. "But I think it now has generally been discontinued."

"That's the operation this chap had. He's sort of a zombie. I can't find out too much about him. Anyhow, Marline knew your man Irving over in Paris. Probably when Marline is freed of responsibilities and gets dolled up in glad rags she's quite a number."

"How about now?" Mason asked.

"Now she's the devoted sister. That's one thing about those French, Perry. They go to town when they're on the loose, but when they assume responsibilities they *really* assume them."

"How long has she been here?" Mason asked.

"She's been in this country for a year, according to her statements to tradesmen. But we haven't been able to check up. She's new in the neighborhood. She moved into her house there when she knew that her brother was coming home. She was living in an apartment up to that time. An apartment house would be a poor place to have a mental case. Marline knew it, so she got this bungalow."

"Living there alone with her brother?"

"A housekeeper comes in part of the day."

"And Irving has been going there?"

"Uh huh. Twice to my knowledge."

"Trying to get Marline to go out?"

"What he's *trying* to get is a question. Marline seems to be very devoted to her brother and very domesticated. The first time my operative shadowed Irving to the place it was in the afternoon. When Marline came to the door there was an affectionate greeting. Irving went inside, stayed for about an hour, and when he left, seemed to be trying to persuade Marline to come with him. He stood in the doorway talking to her. She smiled but kept shaking her head.

"So Irving went away. He was back that night, went inside the house, and apparently Marline sold him on the

65

idea of brother sitting because Marline went out and was gone for an hour or two."

"How did she go?"

"By bus."

"She doesn't have a car?"

"Apparently not."

"Where did she go?"

"Gosh, Perry! You didn't tell me you wanted me to shadow *her*. Do you want me to?"

"No," Mason said, "I guess not, Paul. But the thing interests me. What's happened since?"

"Well, apparently Irving recognized the futility of trying to woo Marline away from her responsibilities, or else the trouble Jefferson is in is weighing heavily on his shoulders. He's keeping pretty much to himself in his apartment now."

"What apartment?" Mason asked.

"The Alta Loma Apartments."

"Pick up anything about the case, Paul?"

"The D.A. is supposed to be loaded for bear on this one. He's so darned anxious to get at you, he's running around in circles. He's told a couple of friendly reporters that this is the sort of case he's been looking for and waiting for. Perry, are you all right on this case?"

"What do you mean, 'all right'?"

"Are *you* in the clear?"

"Sure."

"You haven't been cutting any corners?"

Mason shook his head.

"The D.A. is acting as though he had you where he wanted you. He's like a kid with a new toy for Christmas—a whole Christmas tree full of new toys."

"I'm glad he's happy," Mason said. "What about this Mae Jordan, Paul?"

"I didn't get a lot more than I told you over the phone, except that she's promised to be there at six tonight."

"She's working?"

"That's right."

"What kind of an impression does she make, Paul?"

"Clean-cut and competent," Drake said. "She has a nice voice, nice personality, very neat in her appearance, knows what she's doing every minute of the time, and she certainly can type. Her shorthand is just about as fast as you'd find anywhere."

"She's happy in her job?"

"Apparently not. I don't know what it's all about, but she wants to get away from her present environment."

"Perhaps a thwarted love affair?"

"Could be."

"Sounds like it," Mason said.

"Well, you can find out tonight," Drake told him.

"When we get her into that office tonight, Paul," Mason said, "don't mention my name. Don't make *any* introductions. Simply state that I am the man for whom she will be working."

"Will she recognize you?" Drake asked.

"I don't think I've ever seen her," Mason said, glancing at Della Street.

"That doesn't necessarily mean anything. Your pictures get in the paper a lot."

"Well, if she recognizes me it won't make any difference," Mason said, "because outside of the first few questions, Paul, I'm not going to be talking to her about a job."

"You mean that she'll know the thing was a plant as soon as you walk in?"

"Well, I hope not quite *that* soon," Mason said. "But she'll know it shortly after I start questioning her. As long as she talks I'm going to let her talk."

"That won't be long," Drake said. "She answers questions, but she doesn't volunteer any information."

"All right," Mason said. "I'll see you a little before six tonight, Paul."

"Now remember," Drake warned, "there may be a little trouble."

"How come?"

"This girl has got her mind all set on a job where she can

travel. She wants to get away from everything. The minute you let her know that you were simply locating her as a witness, she's going to resent it."

"What do you think she'll do?" Mason asked.

"She may do anything."

"I'd like that, Paul."

"You would."

"Yes," Mason said. "I'd like to know just what she does when she's good and angry. Don't kid yourself about this girl, Paul. She's mixed up in something pretty sinister."

"How deep is she mixed up in it?"

"Probably up to her eyebrows," Mason said. "This Marline Chaumont knew Walter Irving in Paris?"

"Apparently so. She was sure glad to see him. When he rang the bell and she came to the door, she took one look, then made a flying leap into his arms. She was all French."

"And Irving doesn't go there any more?"

Drake shook his head.

"What would she do if I went out to talk with her this afternoon?"

"She might talk. She might not."

"Would she tell Irving I'd been there?"

"Probably."

"Well, I'll have to take that chance, Paul. I'm going to call on Marline Chaumont."

"May I suggest that you take me?" Della Street asked.

"As a chaperon or for the purpose of keeping notes on what is said?" Mason asked.

"I can be very effective in both capacities," Della Street observed demurely.

"It's that French background," Drake said, grinning. "It scares the devil out of them, Perry."

Chapter 10

Perry Mason drove slowly along Ponce de Leon Drive.

"That's it," Della Street said. "The one on the left, the white bungalow with the green trim."

Mason drove the car past the house, sizing it up, went to the next intersection, made a *U* turn, and drove back.

"What are you going to tell her?" Della Street asked.

"It'll depend on how she impresses me."

"And on how we impress her?"

"I suppose so."

"Isn't this somewhat dangerous, Chief?"

"In what way?"

"She'll be almost certain to tell Irving."

"Tell him what?"

"That you were out checking up on him."

"I'll tell him that myself."

"And then he'll know that you've had people shadowing him."

"If he's known Miss Chaumont in Paris, he won't know just *how* we checked up. I'd like to throw a scare into Mr. Walter Irving. He's too damned sure of himself."

Mason walked up the three steps to the front porch and pushed the bell button.

After a moment the door was opened a cautious three inches. A brass guard chain stretched taut across the opening.

Mason smiled at the pair of bright black eyes which surveyed him from the interior of the house. "We're looking for a Miss Chaumont."

"I am Miss Chaumont."

"Of Paris?"

"Mais oui. I have lived in Paris, yes. Now I live here."

"Would you mind if I asked you a few questions?"

"About what?"

"About Paris?"

"I would love to have you ask me questions about Paris."

"It's rather awkward, standing out here and talking through the door," Mason said.

"Monsieur can hear me?"

"Oh, yes."

"And I can hear you."

Mason smiled at her. Now that his eyes were becoming accustomed to the half-light he could see the oval of the face and a portion of a trim figure.

"Were you familiar with the South African Gem Importing and Exploration Company in Paris?"

"Why do you ask me that question?"

"Because I am interested."

"And who are you?"

"My name is Perry Mason. I am a lawyer."

"Oh, *you* are Perry Mason?"

"That's right."

"I have read about you."

"That's interesting."

"What do you want, Mr. Mason?"

"To know if you knew of the company in Paris."

"I have known of the company, yes."

"And you knew some of the people who worked for that company?"

"But of course, Monsieur. One does not become, as you say, familiar with a company, *non.* One can only become familiar with people, with some of the people, yes? With the company, *non.*"

"Did you know Walter Irving while you were in Paris?"

"Of course. He was my friend. He is here now."

"You went out with him occasionally in Paris?"

"But yes. Is that wrong?"

"No, no," Mason said. "I am simply trying to get the background. Did you know Duane Jefferson?"

"Duane Jefferson is from the South African office. Him I do not know."

"Did you know anyone from the South African office?"

"Twice, when people would come to visit in Paris, they asked me to help . . . well, what you call, entertain. I put on a daring dress. I act wicked with the eyes. I make of them . . . what you call the visiting fireman, *non?*"

"And who introduced you to these men?"

"My friend, Walter."

"Walter Irving?"

"That is right."

"I would like to find out something about Mr. Irving."

"He is nice. Did he tell you I am here?"

"No. I located you through people who work for me. They have an office in Paris."

"And the Paris office locates me here? Monsieur, it is impossible!"

Mason smiled. "I am here."

"And *I* am here. But . . . well, a man of your position, Monsieur Mason, one does not—how you call it?—contradict."

"What sort of a fellow is Walter Irving?"

"Walter Irving has many friends. He is very nice. He has—how you say?—the too big heart. That big heart, she is always getting him in trouble. He gives you too much . . . the shirt off his back. When he trusts, he trusts, that one. Sometime people, they take advantage of him. You are his friend, Monsieur Mason?"

"I would like to know about him."

"This woman with you is your wife?"

"My secretary."

"Oh, a thousand pardons. You seem . . . well, you seem as one."

"We have worked together for a long time."

"I see. Could I say something to you as the friend of Walter Irving?"

"Why not?"

"This Duane Jefferson," she said. "Watch him."

"What do you mean?"

"I mean he is the one to watch. He is sharp. He is very smooth. He . . . he is filled with crazy ideas in his head."

"What do you know about him?"

"*Know*, Monsieur? I *know* but little. But a woman has intuition. A woman can tell. Walter, I know very well. He is big. He is honest. He is like a dog. He trusts. But Walter likes what you call the show-off, the grandstand. He likes many clothes and to show off the good-looking woman on his arm. He likes crowds. He likes—"

She broke off and laughed. "He is simple, that one, for one who is so smart otherwise. He cares about a girl, that she should make people turn to look when he walks with her. So when I go out with Walter I put on a dress that . . . well, your secretary will know. The curves, yes?"

Della Street nodded.

She laughed very lightly. "Then Walter is very happy. I think, Monsieur Mason, that this Jefferson—"

"But I thought you didn't know Jefferson?"

"I hear people talk, and I listen. At times I have very big ears. And now, Monsieur Mason, you will pardon me, no? I have a brother who is sick in his upstairs. He will get better if he can be kept very quiet and have no excitement. You are nice people, and I would invite you in, but the excitement, no."

"Thank you very much," Mason said. "Does Walter Irving know you are here in the city?"

"Know I am here? Of course, he knows. He has located me. He is very eager, that Walter Irving. And he is nice company. If I did not have my brother, I would put on clothes that show the curves and go with him to the night clubs. That he would love. That also I would like. However, I have responsibilities. I have to stay home. But, Monsieur Mason, please . . . you listen to Marline

Chaumont. This Duane Jefferson, he is very cold, very polished, and treacherous like a snake."

"And if you see Walter Irving, you will tell him we were here?"

"You wish me not to?"

"I don't know," Mason said. "I am simply checking."

"I will make you the bargain, Monsieur Mason. You do not tell Walter Irving what I have said about Duane Jefferson, and I do not say to Walter Irving anything that you are here. We keep this a little secret between us, no?

"But, Monsieur Mason, please, if this Duane Jefferson has done things that are wrong, you see that he does not pull my friend Walter down with him?"

"You think Jefferson did something wrong?"

"I have heard people talk."

"But his company gives him an excellent reputation. His company feels the utmost confidence in his honor and his integrity."

"I have told you, Monsieur Mason, that companies cannot feel; only the people in the companies. And later on, when the case comes to trial, Monsieur Mason, I shall read the papers with much interest. But you watch closely this Duane Jefferson. Perhaps he will tell you a story that is very fine as stories go when you do not question, but when he gets on the witness stand and finds that he cannot use the cold English manner to hide behind, then perhaps he gets mad, and when he gets mad, poof! Look out!"

"He has a temper?" Mason asked.

"That, Monsieur Mason, I do not know, but I have heard what others say. He is bad when he gets mad. His manner is a mask."

"I thank you," Mason said.

She hesitated a moment, then archly blew him a kiss with the tips of her fingers. The door closed gently but firmly.

Chapter 11

Perry Mason and Paul Drake left the elevators, walked down the corridor of the big office building.

"Here's the suite," Drake said, pausing in front of a door which had on its frosted glass only the single word "Enter" and the number 555.

Drake opened the door.

"Well," Mason said, looking around, "you certainly fixed up a place here, Paul."

"Rental of desks and chairs," Drake said. "Rental of typewriters. The rest of it all came with the furnished office."

"I didn't know you could rent places like this," Mason said.

"This building caters to an international clientele," Drake explained. "Occasionally they need a large furnished office for directors' meetings, conferences, and things of that sort. The last time this was rented, which was last week, a big Mexican company had it for a trade conference.

"They expect to lose money on this office, of course, but the international goodwill and the convenience to tenants in the building who have big meetings from time to time are supposed to more than offset the loss. Come on in here, Perry."

Drake led the way into a private office.

"This where the interviews take place?" Mason asked.

"That's right."

"This girl will be here at six o'clock?"

"Right on the dot. I have an idea that girl prides herself on being prompt and efficient."

"That's the way I had her sized up," Mason said.

"You aren't ready to tell me yet how you got a line on her?"

"No."

"Or what she has to do with the case?"

Mason said, "She *may* be the girl who made the surreptitious entry into the offices of the South African Gem Importing and Exploration Company."

"I surmised that," Drake said. "It's almost the same description that the police had."

"You have a tape recorder connected?" Mason asked.

"This room is bugged with three microphones," Drake told him. "There's a tape recorder in that closet."

"And what about a receptionist?" Mason asked.

"My receptionist is coming in to—" He broke off as a buzzer sounded. "That means someone's coming in."

Drake got up, went out into the big reception room, came back in a moment with a very attractive young woman.

"Meet Nora Pitts, Perry. She's one of my operatives, working as a receptionist here, and she really knows the ropes."

Miss Pitts, blushing and somewhat flustered, came forward to give Perry Mason her hand.

"I'd been hoping I'd meet you on one of these jobs, Mr. Mason," she said. "Mr. Drake keeps me for the office type of work. Usually I'm on stake-outs. I was beginning to be afraid I was just *never* going to meet you."

"You shouldn't hold out on me like this, Paul," Mason said to the detective.

Drake grinned, looked at his wrist watch, said, "You understand the setup, Nora?"

She nodded.

"Do you know Della Street, my secretary?" Mason asked.

"I know her by sight, yes."

"Well," Mason said, "after this girl has been in here for a few minutes, Miss Street is going to come in. I told her to be here promptly at fifteen minutes past six."

Nora was listening now, her personal reaction at meeting Mason completely subdued by professional concentration.

"What do I do?" she asked.

"I think that this girl will be here by six o'clock, or at least a couple of minutes past six," Mason said. "You send her in as soon as she arrives. I'll start talking with her and questioning her. Della Street will be in at six-fifteen on the dot. We'll hear the buzzer in the office when the door opens and know that she's here, so there'll be no need for you to notify us. Just have Della sit down and wait. I'll buzz for her when I want her sent in."

"Okay," she said.

"You got it, Nora?" Drake asked.

She nodded. "Of course."

Drake looked at his watch. "Well, it's seven minutes to six. She may come in early. Let's go."

Nora Pitts, with a quick smile at Mason, went back to the reception room.

In the office Drake settled down for a smoke, and Mason joined him with a cigarette.

"The newspapers indicate your client is a cold fish," Drake said.

Mason said irritably, "The guy is trying to protect some girl, and we're not going to get his story out of him until after we've got the story our of this girl."

"And you think Mae Jordon is the girl?"

"I don't know. Could be."

"Suppose she is?"

"Then we'll break her down and get her story."

"What do you propose to do then?"

"We'll get a tape recording," Mason said. "Then I'll go down to the jail, tell Jefferson what I have, and tell him to come clean."

"Then what?"

"Then I'll have his story."

"How's the district attorney going to indentify those diamonds, Perry?"

"I don't know much about the case, Paul, but I do know a

lot about the district attorney. He's been laying for me for years.

"This time he thinks he has me. He must have a pretty good case. But I'm gambling there's a legal point he's overlooked."

"What's the point?"

"The *corpus delicti*."

"You think he can't prove it?"

"How's he going to prove a murder?" Mason asked. "They've never found Munroe Baxter's body. Now then, I can show the jury, by Hamilton Burger's own witnesses, that Munroe Baxter was a clever actor who planned to fake a suicide in order to smuggle in gems. Why wouldn't he fake a murder in order to keep from splitting the profit with his female accomplice?

"I'll tell the jury that it's almost certain Baxter has some new babe he's stuck on, some oo-la-la dish who is ready, able and willing to take Yvonne Manco's place as his female accomplice.

"What would be more likely then that Baxter would pretend he had been murdered, so that Yvonne Manco wouldn't be looking for him with fire in her eye?"

"Well, of course, when you put it that way," Drake said, "I can see the possibilities."

"All right," Mason grinned, "that's the way I'm going to put it to the jury. Hamilton Burger isn't going to have the smooth, easy sailing he's anticipating. He'll surprise me. I'll concede he must have something that will hit me hard, but after that, we're going to get down to fundamentals. He can hurt me, but I don't think he can do any more than that. I can blast his case out of court."

They smoked in silence for a few minutes, then Mason said, "What time have you got, Paul? I have five minutes *past* six."

"I have six minutes past, myself," Drake said. "What do you suppose has happened?"

"Do you think she's changed her mind?" Mason asked.

"Hell, no! She was too eager."

Mason began to pace the floor, looking from time to time at his watch.

Promptly at six-fifteen the buzzer sounded.

Mason opened the door to the reception room, said, "Hello, Della. Come in."

Della Street entered the private office. "No typist?" she asked.

"No typist," Mason said.

"Suppose it's simply a case of her being delayed or—"

Mason shook his head. "That girl wasn't delayed. She has become suspicious."

"Not while she was here," Drake said positively. "When she left the place, her eyes were shining. She—"

"Sure," Mason said. "But she's smart. She went to the Better Business Bureau or a credit agency and got somebody to call up the office of this building and find out who was renting this office."

"Oh-oh!" Drake exclaimed.

"You mean you left a back trail?" Mason asked.

"I had to, Perry. If she went at it that way, she could have found out this office was being rented by the Drake Detective Agency."

Mason grabbed for his hat. "Come on, Paul. Let's go."

"Want me?" Della Street asked.

Mason hesitated, then said, "You may as well come on, and we'll buy you a dinner afterward."

Mason paused in the big reception office only long enough to tell Nora Pitts to stay on the job until Drake phoned.

"If that girl comes in, hold her," Drake said. "Keep her here and phone the office."

They got in Mason's car. Mason drove to the address on Cabachon Street, which was a narrow-fronted, two-story apartment house.

"Apartment two-eighteen," Drake said.

Mason repeatedly jabbed the button. When there was no answer he rang the bell for the manager.

The door latch clicked open. Drake held the door open.

They went in. The manager, a big-boned woman in her sixties, came out to look them over. She studied the group with a cold, practiced eye. "We have no short-term rentals," she said.

Drake said, "I'm an investigator. We're looking for information. We're trying to locate Mae Jordan."

"Oh, yes," the woman said. "Well, Miss Jordan left."

"What do you mean she left?"

"Well, she told me she'd be away for a while and asked me if I'd feed her canary."

"She was going somewhere?"

"I guess so. She seemed in a terrific hurry. She dashed into the apartment and packed a couple of suitcases."

"Was she alone?" Mason asked.

"No. Two men were with her."

"Two men."

"That's right."

"Did she introduce them?"

"No."

"They went up to the apartment with her?"

"Yes."

"And came down with her?"

"Yes. Each one of them was carrying a suitcase."

"And Miss Jordan didn't tell you how long she'd be gone?"

"No."

"How did she come here? Was it in a car or a taxi-cab?"

"I didn't see her come, but she left in a private car with these two men. Why? Is there anything wrong?"

Mason exchanged glances with Paul Drake.

"What time was this?" Mason asked.

"About . . . oh, let's see . . . It's been a little over an hour and a half, I guess."

"Thank you," Mason said, and led the way back to the car.

"Well?" Drake asked.

"Start your men going, Paul," Mason said. "Find out

where Mae Jordan worked. Get the dope on her. Dig up everything you can. I want that girl."

"What are you going to do with her when you get her?" Drake asked.

"I'm going to slap her with a subpoena, put her on the witness stand, and tear her insides out," Mason said grimly. "How long will it take you to find out where Walter Irving is right now?"

"I'll know as soon as my operatives phone in the next report. I've got two men on the job. Generally, they phone in about once an hour."

"When you locate him, let me know," Mason said. "I'll be in my office."

Della Street smiled at Paul Drake. "Dinner," she said, "has been postponed."

Chapter 12

Mason had been in his office less than ten minutes when the unlisted phone rang. Della Street glanced inquiringly at Mason. The lawyer said, "I'll take it, Della," and picked up the phone.

"Hello, Paul. What is it?"

Drake said, "One of my operatives reported Irving is on his way to this building, and he's hopping mad."

"To *this* building?"

"That's right."

"That leaves three objectives," Mason said. "His office, your office, or mine. If he comes to your office send him in here."

"If he comes to your office, will you want help?"

"I'll handle it," Mason said.

"My operative says he's really breathing fire. He got a phone call when he was right in the middle of dinner. He never even went back to his table. Just dashed out, grabbed a cab, and gave the address of this building."

"Okay," Mason said. "We'll see what develops."

Mason hung up the telephone and said to Della Street, "Irving is on his way here."

"To see you?"

"Probably."

"So what do we do?"

"Wait for him. The party may be rough."

Five minutes later angry knuckles banged on the door of Mason's private office. "That will be Irving," Mason said. "I'll let him in myself, Della."

Mason got up, strode across the office and jerked the door open.

"Good evening," he said coldly, his face granite hard.

"What the hell are you trying to do?" Irving asked furiously. "Upset the apple cart?"

Mason said, "There are ladies present. Watch your language unless you want to get thrown out."

"Who's going to throw me out?"

"I am."

"You and who else?"

"Just me."

Irving sized him up for a moment. "You're one hell of a lawyer, I'll say that for you."

"All right," Mason told him. "Come in. Sit down. Tell me what's on your mind. And the next time you try to hold out anything on me, you'll be a lot sorrier than you are right now."

"I wasn't holding out on you. I—"

"All right," Mason told him. "Tell me *your* troubles, and then *I'll* tell *you* something."

"You went out to call on Marline Chaumont."

"Of course I did."

"You shouldn't have done it."

"Then why didn't you tell me so?"

"To tell you the truth, I didn't think you could possibly find out anything about her. I still don't know how you did it."

"Well, what's wrong with going to see her?" Mason asked.

"You've kicked your case out of the window, that's all that's wrong with it."

"Go on. Tell me the rest of it."

"I'd been nursing that angle of the case until I could get the evidence we needed. She was pulling this gag of having an invalid brother on her hands so she—"

"That's a gag?" Mason interrupted.

"Don't be any simpler than you have to be," Irving snapped.

"What about her brother?" Mason asked.

"Her brother!" Irving stormed. "Her brother! You poor,

simple-minded boob! Her so-called brother is Munroe
Baxter.''

"Go on," Mason said. "Keep talking."

"Isn't that fact enough to show you what you've done?"

"The fact would be. Your statement isn't."

"Well, I'm telling you."

"You've told me. I don't want your guesses or surmises.
I want facts."

"Marline is a smart little babe. She's French. She's chic,
and she's a fast thinker. She's been playing around with
Munroe Baxter. He likes her better than Yvonne Manco. He
was beginning to get tired of Yvonne.

"So when Munroe Baxter took the nose dive, he just kept
on diving and came up into the arms of Marline Chaumont.
She had a home all prepared for him as the invalid brother
who was weak in the upper story."

"Any proof?" Mason asked.

"I was getting proof."

"You've seen Marline?"

"Of course I've seen her. After I got to thinking things
over, I made it a point to see her."

"And did you see her brother?"

"I tried to," Irving said, "but she was too smart for me.
She had him locked in a back bedroom, and she had the
only key. She wanted to go to the all-night bank and transact
some business. I told her I'd stay with her brother. She took
me up on it.

"After she was gone, I prowled the house. The back
bedroom was locked. I think she'd given him a sedative or
something. I could hear him gently snoring. I knocked on
the door and tried to wake him up. I wanted to look at him."

"You think he's Munroe Baxter?"

"I know he's Munroe Baxter."

"How do you know it?"

"I don't have to go into that with you."

"The hell you don't!"

Irving shrugged his shoulders. "You've started messing
the case up now. Go ahead and finish it."

"All right, I will," Mason said. "I'll put that house under surveillance. I'll—"

"You and your house under surveillance!" Irving exclaimed scornfully. "Marline and her 'brother' got out of there within thirty minutes after you left the place. That house is as cold and dead as a last-year's bird's nest. In case you want to bet, I'll give you ten to one you can't find a fingerprint in the whole damn place."

"Where did they go?" Mason asked.

Irving shrugged his shoulders. "Search me. I went out there. The place was empty. I became suspicious and got a private detective agency to get on the job and find out what had happened. I was eating dinner tonight when the detective phoned. Neighbors had seen a car drive up. A man and a woman got out. A neighbor was looking through the curtains. She recognized you from your pictures. The description of the girl with you checked with that of your secretary here, Miss Street.

"Half an hour after you left, a taxi drove up. Marline sent out four big suitcases and a handbag. Then she and the taxi driver helped a man out to the car. The man was stumbling around as though he was drunk or drugged or both."

"And then?" Mason asked.

"The cab drove away."

"All right," Mason said. "We'll trace that cab."

Irving laughed scornfully. "You must think you're dealing with a bunch of dumb bunnies, Mason."

"Perhaps I am," Mason said.

"Go on and try to trace that couple," he said. "Then you'll find out what a mess you've made of things."

Irving got to his feet.

"How long had you known all this?" Mason asked, his voice ominously calm.

"Not long. I looked Marline up when I came here. She knows everyone in the Paris office. She was our party girl. She always helped in entertaining buyers.

"She's smart. She got wise to the Baxter deal and she put the heat on Baxter.

"As soon as I went out to Marline's place to call on her, I knew something was wrong. She went into a panic at the sight of me. She tried to cover up by being all honey and syrup, but she overdid it. She had to invite me in, but she told me this story about her brother. Then she kept me waiting while she locked him up and knocked him out with a hypo. That evening she left me alone, so I could prowl the house. Baxter was dead to the world. She's a smart one, that girl.

"I was getting ready to really bust this case wide open, and then you had to stick your clumsy hand right in the middle of all the machinery."

Irving started for the door.

"Wait a minute," Mason said. "You're not finished yet. You know something more about all—"

"Sure I do," Irving said. "And make no mistake, Mason. What I know I keep to myself from now on. In case you're interested, I'm cabling the company to kiss their two-thousand-dollar retainer good-by and to hire a lawyer who at least has *some* sense."

Irving strode out into the corridor.

Della Street watched the closing door. When it had clicked shut she started for the telephone.

Mason motioned her away. "Remember, it's all taken care of, Della," he said. "Paul Drake has two men shadowing him. We'll know where he goes when he leaves here."

"That's fine," she said. "In that case, you can take me to dinner now."

Chapter 13

Della Street laid the decoded cablegram on Mason's desk as the lawyer entered the office.

"What's this, Della?" Mason asked, hanging up his hat.

"Cablegram from the South African Gem Importing and Exploration Company."

"Am I fired?"

"Definitely not."

"What does it say?" Mason asked.

"It says you are to continue with the case and to protect the interests of Duane Jefferson, that the company investigated you before you were retained, that it has confidence in you, and that its official representative in this area, and the only one in a position to give orders representing the company, is Duane Jefferson."

"Well," Mason said, "that's something." He took the decoded cablegram and studied it. "It sounds as though they didn't have too much confidence in Walter Irving."

"Of course," she told him, "we don't know what Irving cabled the company."

"We know what he told us he was cabling the company."

"Where does all this leave him?" Della Street asked.

"Out on a limb," Mason said, grinning, and then added, "It also leaves us out on a limb. If we don't get some line on Mae Jordan and Marline Chaumont, we're behind the eight ball."

"Couldn't you get a continuance under the circumstances until—"

Mason shook his head.

"Why not, Chief?"

"For several reasons," Mason said. "One of them is that

I assured the district attorney I'd got to trial on the first date we could squeeze in on the trial calender. The other is that I still think we have more to gain than to lose by getting to trial before the district attorney has had an opportunity to think over the real problem."

"Do you suppose this so-called brother of Marline Chaumont is really Munroe Baxter?"

Mason looked at his watch, said, "Paul Drake should have the answer to that by this time. Get him on the phone, Della. Ask him to come in."

Ten minutes later Paul Drake was laying it on the line.

"This guy Irving is all wet, Perry. Marline Chaumont showed up at the state hospital. She identified herself as the sister of Pierre Chaumont. Pierre had been there for a year. He'd become violent. The'd operated on his brain. After that, he was like a pet dog. He was there because there was no other place for him to be. Authorities were very glad to release Pierre to his sister, Marline. The chance that he is Munroe Baxter is so negligible you can dismiss it.

"In the first place, Marline showed up and got him out of the state hospital more than a month before Baxter's boat was due. At the time Marline was getting him out of the hospital, Munroe Baxter was in Paris."

"Is his real name Pierre Chaumont?"

"The authorities are satisfied it is."

"Who satisfied them?"

"I don't know; Marline, I guess. The guy was going under another name. He'd been a vicious criminal, a psychopath. He consented to having this lobotomy performed, and they did it. It apparently cured him of his homicidal tendencies, but it left him like a zombie. As I understand it, he's in sort of a hypnotic trance. Tell the guy anything, and he does it."

"You checked with the hospital?"

"With everyone. The doctor isn't very happy about the outcome. He said he had hoped for better results, but the guy was a total loss the way he was and anything is an improvement. They were damn glad to get rid of him at the hospital."

"Yes, I can imagine. What else, Paul?"

"Now here's some news that's going to jolt you, Perry."

"Go ahead and jolt."

"Mae Jordan was picked up by investigators from the district attorney's office."

"The hell!" Mason exclaimed.

Drake nodded.

"What are they trying to do? Get a confession of some sort out of her?"

"Nobody knows. Two men showed up at the law office where she works yesterday afternoon. It took me a while to get the name of that law office, but I finally got it. It's one of the most substantial, conservative firms in town, and it created quite a furor when these two men walked in, identified themselves and said they wanted Mae Jordan.

"They had a talk with her in a private office, then came out and hunted up old man Honcut, who's the senior member of the firm Honcut, Gridley and Billings. They told him that for Mae's own safety they were going to have to keep her out of circulation for a while. She had about three weeks for vacation coming, and they told Honcut she could come back right after the trial."

"She went willingly?" Mason asked.

"Apparently so."

Mason thought that over. "How did they find her, Paul?"

"Simplest thing in the word. They searched Jefferson when they booked him. There was a name and address book. It was all in code. They cracked the code and ran down the names. When they came to this Jordan girl she talked."

"She tried to talk herself out by talking Duane Jefferson in," Mason said grimly. "When that young woman gets on the stand she's going to have a cross-examination she'll remember for a long, long time. What about Irving, Paul? Where did he go after he left here?"

"Now there," Drake said, "I have some more bad news for you."

Mason's face darkened. "That was damn important, Paul. I told you—"

"I know what you *told* me, Perry. Now *I'm* going to tell *you* something about the shadowing business that I've told you a dozen times before and I'll probably tell you a dozen times again. If a smart man knows he's being tailed and doesn't want to be shadowed, there's not much you can do about it. If he's smart, he can give you the slip every time, unless you have four or five operatives all equipped with some means of intercommunication."

"But Irving didn't *know* he was being tailed."

"What makes you think he didn't?"

"Well," Mason said, "he didn't act like it when he came up here to the office?"

"He sure acted like it when he left," Drake said. "What did you tell him?"

"Nothing to arouse his suspicions. Specifically, what did he do, Paul?"

"He proceeded to ditch the shadows."

"How?"

"To begin with, he got a taxi. He must have told the taxi driver there was a car following him that he wanted to ditch. The cab driver played smart. He'd slide up to the traffic signals just as they were changing, then go on through. My man naturally tried to keep up with him, relying on making an explanation to any traffic cop who might stop him.

"Well, a traffic cop stopped him and it happened he was a cop who didn't feel kindly toward private detectives. He got tough, held my man, and gave him a ticket. By that time, Irving was long since gone.

"Usually a cop will give you a break on a deal like that if you have your credentials right handy, show them to him and tell him you're shadowing the car ahead. This chap deliberately held my man up until Irving got away. Not that I think it would have made any difference. Irving knew that he was being tailed, and he'd made up his mind he was going to ditch the tail. When a smart man gets an idea like that in his head, there's nothing you can do about it except roll with the punch and take it."

"So what did you do, Paul?"

"Did the usual things. Put men on his apartment house to pick him up when he got back. Did everything."

"And he hasn't been back?"

Drake shook his head.

"All right. What about the others?"

"Marline Chaumont," Drake said. "You thought it would be easy to locate her."

"You mean you've drawn a blank all the way along the line?" Mason interposed impatiently.

"I found out about Mae Jordan," Drake said.

"And that's all?"

"That's all."

"All right. What about Marline Chaumont? Give me the bad news in bunches."

"It took me a devil of a time to find the taxicab driver who went out to the house," Drake said. "I finally located him. He remembered the occasion well. He took the woman, the man, four suitcases and a handbag to the airport."

"And then what?" Mason asked.

"Then we draw a blank. We can't find where she left the airport."

"You mean a woman with a man who is hardly able to navigate by himself, with four big suitcases and a handbag, can vanish from the airport?" Mason asked.

"That's right," Drake said. "Just try it sometime, Perry."

"Try what?"

"Covering all of the taxicab drivers who go to the air terminal. Try and get them to tell you whether they picked up a man, a woman, four suitcases and a handbag. People are coming in by plane every few minutes. The place is a regular madhouse."

Mason thought that over. "All right, Paul," he said.

"Irving told me we'd get no place, but I thought the four suitcases would do it."

"So did I when you first told me about it," Drake said.

"They went directly to the airport?"

"That's right."

"Paul, they must have gone *somewhere*."

"Sure, they went somewhere," Drake said. "I can tell you where they *didn't* go."

"All right. Where didn't they go?"

"They didn't take any plane that left at about that time of day."

"How do you know?"

"I checked it by the excess baggage. The taxi driver says the suitcases were heavy. They must have weighed forty pounds each. I checked the departures on the planes."

"You checked them by name, of course?"

Drake's look was withering. "Don't be silly, Perry. That was the first thing. That was simple. Then I checked with the ticket sellers to see if there was a record of tickets sold at that time of day with that amount of excess baggage. There wasn't. Then I checked with the gate men to see if they remembered some woman going through the gate who would need help in getting a man aboard the plane. There was none. I also checked on wheel chairs. No dice. So then I concluded she'd gone to the airport, unloaded, paid off the cab, and had picked up another cab at the airport to come back."

"And you couldn't find that cab?"

"My men are still working on it. But that's like going to some babe wearing a skirt reaching to her knees, a tight sweater, and asking her if she remembered anybody whistling at her yesterday as she walked down the street."

After a moment Mason grinned. "All right, Paul. We're drawing a blank. Now why the devil would the district attorney have Mae Jordan picked up?"

"Because he wanted to question her."

"Then why wouldn't he have let her go after he questioned her?"

"Because he hasn't finished questioning her."

Mason shook his head. "You overlook what happened. She went up to her room, packed—got two suitcases. The district attorney is keeping her in what amounts to custody."

"Why?"

Mason grinned. "Now wait a minute, Paul. That's the question that I asked you. Of course, the only answer is that he wants her as a material witness. But if he does that, it means she must have told a story that has pulled the wool completely over his eyes, and he fell for it hook, line, and sinker."

"You don't think she's a material witness?" Drake asked.

Mason thought the situation over for a minute, then a slow smile spread over his features. "She would be, if she told the truth. I don't think there's any better news that I could have had."

"Why?"

"Because if the district attorney doesn't put her on the stand as a witness, I'll claim that he sabotaged my case by spiriting away *my* witnesses. If he does put her on the stand, I'll make him the sickest district attorney west of Chicago."

"You're going to play into his hands by going to an immediate trial?" Drake asked.

Mason grinned. "Paul, did you ever see a good tug of war?"

Drake thought for a moment, then said, "They used to put them on in the country towns on the Fourth of July."

"And did you ever see the firemen having a tug of war with the police department?"

"I may have. I can't remember. Why?"

"And," Mason went on, "about the time the fire department was all dug in and huffing and puffing, there would be a secret signal from the police department and everybody would give the firemen a lot of slack and they'd go over backwards, and then the police department would give a big yo-heave-ho and pull the whole aggregation right over the dividing line on the seat of their pants."

Drake ginned. "Seems to me I remember something like that, now that you speak of it."

"Well," Mason said, "that is what is known as playing into the hands of the district attorney, Paul. We're going to give him lots of slack. Now, answering your question more specifically—yes, I'm going to an immediate trial. I'm going to go to trial while the D.A. is hypnotized by Mae Jordan's story and before he finds out I know some of the things I know and that he doesn't know."

Chapter 14

The selection of the jury was completed at ten-thirty on the second day of the trial. Judge Hartley settled back on the bench, anticipating a long, bitterly contested trial.

"Gentlemen," he said, "the jury has been selected and sworn. The prosecution will proceed with its opening statement."

At that moment, Hamilton Burger, the district attorney, who had left the selection of the jury to subordinates, dramatically strode into the courtroom to take charge of the trial personally.

The district attorney bowed to the judge and, almost without pausing, passed the counsel table to stand facing the jury.

"Good morning, ladies and gentlemen of the jury," he said. "I am the district attorney of this county. We expect to show you that the defendant in this case is an employee of the South African Gem Importing and Exploration Company; that through his employment he had reason to know that man named Munroe Baxter had in his possession a large number of diamonds valued at more than three hundred thousand dollars on the retail market; that the defendant knew Munroe Baxter intended to smuggle those diamonds into this country, and that the defendant murdered Munroe Baxter and took possession of those diamonds. We will introduce witnesses to show premeditation, deliberation and the cunning execution of a diabolical scheme of murder. We will show that a goodly proportion of the diamonds smuggled into the country by Munroe Baxter were found in the possession of the defendant. On the strength of that evidence we shall ask for a verdict of first-degree murder."

And Hamilton Burger, bowing to the jury, turned and stalked back to the counsel table.

Court attachés looked at each other in surprise. It was the shortest opening statement Hamilton Burger had ever made, and no one missed its significance. Hamilton Burger had carefully refrained from disclosing his hand or giving the defense the faintest inkling of how he intended to prove his case.

"My first witness," Hamilton Burger said, "will be Yvonne Manco."

"Come forward, Yvonne Manco," the bailiff called.

Yvonne Manco had evidently been carefully instructed. She came forward, trying her best to look demure. Her neckline was high and her skirt was fully as long as the current styles dictated, but the attempt to make her look at all conservative was as unsuccessful as would have been an attempt to disguise a racing sports car as a family sedan.

Yvonne gave her name and address to the court reporter, then looked innocently at the district attorney—after having flashed a sidelong glance of appraisal at the men of the jury.

Under questioning of the district attorney, Yvonne told the story of her relationship with Munroe Baxter, of the carefully laid plot to smuggle the gems, of the tour aboard the cruise ship, the spurious "whirlwind courtship."

She told of the plot to arrange the fake suicide, her deliberate flirtation with the assistant purser, the scene on the ship, and then finally that early morning plunge into the waters of the bay. She disclosed that she had carried a small compressed air tank in her baggage and that when Baxter went overboard, he was prepared to swim for a long distance underwater.

Hamilton Burger brought out a series of maps and photographs of the cruise ship. He had the witness indentify the approximate place where the leap had taken place, both from the deck of the streamer and from its location in the bay.

"You may cross-examine," he said to Perry Mason.

Mason smiled at the witness, who promptly returned his

smile, shifted her position slightly and crossed her legs, so that two of the masculine members of the jury hitched forward in their chairs for a better look, while the chins of two of the less attractive women on the jury were conspicuously elevated.

"You go by the name of Yvonne Manco?" Mason asked.

"Yes."

"You have another name?"

"No."

"You were really married to Munroe Baxter, were you not?"

"Yes, but now that I am a widow I choose to keep my maiden name of Yvonne Manco."

"I see," Mason said. "You don't want to bear the name of your husband?"

"It is not that," she said. "Yvonne Manco is my professional name."

"What profession?" Mason asked.

There was a moment's silence, then Hamilton Burger was on his feet. "Your Honor, I object. I object to the manner in which the question is asked. I object to the question. Incompetent, irrelevant, and immaterial."

Judge Hartley stroked his chin thoughtfully. "Well," he said, "under the circumstances I'm going to sustain the objection. However, in view of the answer of the witness— However, the objection is sustained."

"You were, however, married to Munroe Baxter?"

"Yes."

"On shipboard?"

"Yes."

"Before that?"

"No."

"There had been no previous ceremony?"

"No."

"Are you familiar with what is referred to as a common law marriage?"

"Yes."

"Had you ever gone by the name of Mrs. Baxter?"

"Yes."

"Prior to this cruise?"

"Yes."

"As a part of this plot which you and Munroe Baxter hatched up, he was to pretend to be dead. Is that right?"

"Yes."

"With whom did the idea originate? You or Munroe Baxter?"

"With him."

"He was to pretend to jump overboard and be dead, so he could smuggle in some diamonds?"

"Yes. I have told you this."

"In other words," Mason said, "if at any time it should be to his advantage, he was quite willing to pretend to be dead."

"Objected to as calling for the conclusion of the witness as already asked and answered," Hamilton Burger said.

"Sustained," Judge Hartley said.

Mason, having made his point, smiled at the jury. "You knew that you were engaging in a smuggling transaction?" he asked the witness.

"But of course. I am not stupid."

"Exactly," Mason said. "And after this investigation started, you had some contact with the district attorney?"

"Naturally."

"And was it not through the offices of the district attorney that arrangements were made so you could testify in this case, yet to be held harmless and not be prosecuted for smuggling?"

"Well, of course—"

"Just a minute, just a minute," Hamilton Burger interrupted. "I want to interpose an objection to that question, Your Honor."

"Go ahead," Judge Hartley ruled.

"It is incompetent, irrelevant and immaterial. It is not proper cross-examination."

"Overruled," Judge Hartley said. "Answer the question."

"Well, of course there was no definite agreement. That would have been . . . unwise."

"Who told you it would be unwise?"

"It was agreed by all that it would be unwise."

"By all, whom do you mean? Whom do you include?"

"Well, the customs people, the district attorney, the detectives, the police, my own lawyer."

"I see," Mason said. "They told you that it would be unwise to have a definite agreement to this effect, but nevertheless they gave you every assurance that if you testified as they wished, you would not be prosecuted on a smuggling charge?"

"Your Honor, I object to the words 'as they wished,'" Hamilton Burger said. "That calls for a conclusion of the witness."

Judge Hartley looked down at the witness.

Mason said, "I'll put it this way, was there any conversation as to what you were to testify to?"

"The truth."

"Who told you that?"

"Mr. Burger, the district attorney."

"And was there some assurance given you that if you so testified, you would be given immunity from the smuggling?"

"If I testified to the *truth?* Yes."

"Before this assurance was given you, you had told these people what the truth was?"

"Yes."

"And that was the same story you have told on the witness stand here?"

"Certainly."

"So that when the district attorney told you to tell the truth, you understood that he meant the same story you have just told here?"

"Yes."

"So then, the assurance that was given you was that if you would tell the story you have now told on the witness stand, you would be given immunity from smuggling."

"That was my understanding."

"So," Mason said, "simply by telling this story you are given immunity from smuggling?"

"Well, not—It was not that . . . not that crude," she said.

The courtroom broke into laughter.

"That," Mason said, "is all."

Hamilton Burger was plainly irritated as the witness left the stand. "My next witness will be Jack Gilly," he said.

Jack Gilly was a slender, shifty-eyed man with high cheekbones, a long, sharp nose, a high forehead, and a pointed chin. He moved with a silence that was almost furtive as he glided up to the witness stand, held up his hand, was sworn, gave his name and address to the court reporter, seated himself, and looked expectantly at the district attorney.

"What's your occupation?" Hamilton Burger asked.

"At the moment?" he asked.

"Well, do you have the same occupation now you had six months ago?"

"Yes."

"What is it?"

"I rent fishing boats."

"Where?"

"At the harbor here."

"Were you acquainted with Munroe Baxter during his lifetime?"

"Just a moment before you answer that question," Mason said to the witness. He turned to Judge Hartley. "I object, Your Honor, on the ground that the question assumes a fact not in evidence. As far as the evidence before this court at the present time is concerned, Munroe Baxter is still alive."

"May I be heard on that, Your Honor?" Hamilton Bruger asked.

"Well," Judge Hartley said, hesitating, "it would certainly seem that the logical way to present this case would be first to— However, I'll hear you, Mr. District Attorney."

"If the Court please," Hamilton Burger said, "Munroe

Baxter jumped overboard in deep water. He was never seen alive afterward. I have witnesses from the passengers and the crew who will testify that Munroe Baxter ran to the rear of the ship, jumped overboard and vanished in the water. The ship called for a launch to come alongside, the waters were searched and searched carefully. Munroe Baxter never came up."

"Well," Judge Hartley said, "you can't expect this Court to rule on evidence predicated upon an assumption as to what you intend to prove by other witnesses. Moreover, your own witness has testified that this is all part of a scheme on the part of Munroe Baxter to—"

"Yes, yes, I know," Hamilton Burger interrupted. "But schemes can go astray. Many unforeseen things can enter into the picture. Jumping from the deck of a ship is a perilous procedure."

Judge Hartley said, "Counsel will kindly refrain from interrupting the Court. I was about to say, Mr. District Attorney, that the testimony of your own witness indicates this was all part of a planned scheme by which Munroe Baxter intended to appear to commit suicide. In view of the fact that there is a presumption that a man remains alive until he is shown to be dead, the Court feels the objection is well taken."

"Very well, Your Honor, I will reframe the question," Hamilton Burger said. "Mr. Gilly, did you know Munroe Baxter?"

"Yes."

"How well did you know him?"

"I had met him several times."

"Were you acquainted with Yvonne Manco, who has just testified?"

"Yes."

"Directing your attention to the sixth day of June of this year, what was your occupation at that time?"

"I was renting boats."

"And to the fifth day of June, what was your occupation?"

"I was renting boats."

"Did you rent a boat on the fifth of June at an hour nearing seven o'clock in the evening?"

"Yes, sir."

"To whom did you rent that boat?"

"Frankly, I don't know."

"It was to some man you had never seen before?"

"Yes."

"Did the man tell you what he wanted?"

"He said that he had been directed to me because I was—"

"Just a moment," Mason interrupted. "I object to any conversation which did not take place in the presence of the defendant and which is not connected up with the defendant."

"I propose to connect this up with the defendant," Hamilton Burger said.

"Then the connection should be shown before the conversation," Mason said.

Judge Hartley nodded. "The objection is sustained."

"Very well. You rented a boat to this man who was a stranger to you?"

"Yes, sir."

"From what this man said, however, you had reason to rent him the boat?"

"Yes."

"Was money paid you for the boat?"

"Yes."

"And when did the man start out in the boat, that is, when did he take delivery of it?"

"At about five o'clock the next morning."

"What were the circumstances surrounding the delivery of the boat?"

"He stood on the dock with me. I had a pair of powerful night glasses. When I saw the cruise ship coming in the harbor, I said to this man that I could see the cruise ship, and he jumped in the boat and took off."

"Did he start the motor?"

"The motor had been started an hour previously so it would be warm and so everything would be in readiness."

"And what did the man do?"

"He guided the boat away from my dock and out into the channel."

"Just a moment," Mason said. "Your Honor, I move to strike all of this evidence out on the ground that it has not been connected with the defendant in any way."

"I am going to connect it up," Hamilton Burger said, "within the next few questions."

"The Court will reserve a ruling," Judge Hartley said. "It seems to me that these questions are largely preliminary."

"What did *you* do after the boat was rented?" Hamilton Burger asked the witness.

"Well," Gilly said, "I was curious. I wanted to see—"

"Never mind your thoughts or emotions," Hamilton Burger said. "What did you *do?*"

"I walked back to where my car was parked, got in the car and drove out to a place I knew on the waterfront where I could get out on the dock and watch what was going on."

"What do you mean by your words, 'what was going on'?"

"Watch the boat I had rented."

"And what did you see?"

"I saw the cruise ship coming slowly into the harbor."

"And what else did you see?"

"I saw Munroe Baxter jump overboard."

"You know it was Munroe Baxter?"

"Well, I— Of course, I knew it from what happened."

"But did you recognize him?"

"Well . . . it looked like Baxter, but at that distance and in that light I couldn't *swear* to it."

"Don't swear to it then," Hamilton Burger snapped. "You saw a man jump overboard?"

"Yes."

"Did that man look like anyone you knew?"

"Yes."

"Who?"

"Munroe Baxter."

"That is, as I understand your testimony, he looked like Munroe Baxter, but you can't definitely swear that it *was* Munroe Baxter. Is that right?"

"That's right."

"Then what happened?"

"I saw people running around on the deck of the cruise ship. I heard voices evidently hailing a launch, and a launch came and cruised around the ship."

"What else happened?"

"I kept my binoculars trained on the boat I rented."

"What did you see?"

"There were two men in the boat."

"*Two* men?" Hamilton Burger asked.

"Yes, sir."

"Where did the other man come from, do you know?"

"No, sir. I don't. But I am assuming that he was picked up on one of the docks while I was getting my car."

"That may go out," Hamilton Burger said. "You don't know of your own knowledge where this man came from?"

"No, sir."

"You know only that by the time you reached the point of vantage from which you could see the boat, there were two men in the boat?"

"Yes, sir."

"All right, then what happened?"

"The boat sat there for some time. The second man appeared to be fishing. He was holding a heavy bamboo rod and a line over the side of the boat."

"And then what happened?"

"After quite a while I saw the fishing pole suddenly jerk, as though something very heavy had taken hold of the line."

"And then what?"

"Then I could see a black body partially submerged in the water, apparently hanging onto the fish line."

"And then what did you see?"

"One of the men leaned over the side of the boat. He appeared to be talking—"

"Never mind what he appeared to be doing. What did he do?"

"He leaned over the side of the boat."

"Then what?"

"Then he reached down to the dark object in the water."

"Then what?"

"Then I saw him raise his right arm and lower it rapidly several times. There was a knife in his hand. He was plunging the knife down into the dark thing in the water."

"Then what?"

"Then both men fumbled around with the thing that was in the water; then one of the men lifted a heavy weight of some kind over the side of the boat and tied it to the thing that was in the water."

"Then what?"

"Then they started the motor in the boat, slowly towing the weighted object in the water. I ran back to my automobile, got into it and drove back to my boat pier."

"And what happened then?"

"Then after a couple of hours the man who had rented the boat brought it back."

"Was anyone with him at the time?"

"No, sir, he was alone."

"What did you do?"

"I asked him if he had picked anyone up and he—"

"I object to any conversation which was not in the presence of the defendant," Mason said.

"Just a moment," Hamilton Burger said. "I will withdraw the question until I connect it up. Now, Mr. Gilly, did you recognize the other man who was in the boat with this stranger?"

"Not at the time. I had never seen him before."

"Did you see him subsequently?"

"Yes, sir."

"Who was that man?"

"The defendant."

"You are referring now to Duane Jefferson, the defendant who is seated here in the courtroom?"

"Yes, sir."

"Are you positive of your indentification?"

"Just a moment," Mason said. "That's objected to as an attempt on the part of counsel to cross-examine his own witness."

"Overruled," Judge Hartley said. "Answer the question."

"Yes, sir, I am positive."

"You were watching through binoculars?"

"Yes, sir."

"What is the power of those binoculars?"

"Seven by fifty."

"Are they a good pair of binoculars?"

"Yes, sir."

"With coated lenses?"

"Yes, sir."

"You could see the boat clearly enough to distinguish the features of the people who were in the boat?"

"Yes, sir."

"Now then, after the boat was returned to you, did you notice any stains on the boat?"

"Yes, sir."

"What were those stains?"

"Bloodstains that—"

"No, no," Hamilton Burger said. "Just describe the stains. You don't know whether they were blood."

"I know they *looked* like blood."

"Just describe the stains, please," Hamilton Burger insisted, striving to appear virtuous and impartial.

"They were reddish stains, dark reddish stains."

"Where were they?"

"On the side of the boat, just below the gunwale, and over on the inside of the boat where there had been a spattering or spurting."

"When did you first notice those stains?"

"Just after the boat had been returned to me."

"Were they fresh at that time?"

"Objected to as calling for a conclusion of the witness and no proper foundation laid," Mason said.

"The objection is sustained," Judge Hartley ruled.

"Well, how did they appear to you?"

"Same objection."

"Same ruling."

"Look here," Hamilton Burger said, "you have been engaged in the fishing business and in fishing for recreation for some time?"

"Yes, sir."

"During that time you have had occasion to see a lot of blood on boats?"

"Yes, sir."

"And have you been able to judge the relative freshness of the stains by the color of that blood?"

"Yes, sir."

"That's fish blood the witness is being asked about?" Mason interposed.

"Well . . . yes," Hamilton Burger conceded.

"And may I ask the prosecutor if it is his contention that these stains on the boat the witness has described were fish blood?"

"Those were stains of human blood!" Hamilton Burger snapped.

"I submit," Mason said, "that a witness cannot be qualified as an expert on human bloodstains by showing that he has had experience with fish blood."

"The principle is the same," Hamilton Burger said. "The blood assumes the same different shades of color in drying."

"Do I understand the district attorney is now testifying as an expert?" Mason asked.

Judge Hartley smiled. "I think the Court will have to agree with defense counsel, Mr. District Attorney. There must first be a showing as to whether there is a similarity in the appearance of fish blood and human blood *if* you are now trying to qualify this witness as an expert."

"Oh, well," Hamilton Burger said, "I'll get at it in another way by another witness. You are positive as to your indentification of this defendant, Mr. Gilly?"

"Yes, sir."

"And he was in the boat at the time you saw this thing— whatever it was—stabbed with a knife?"

"Yes, sir."

"Were these stains you have mentioned on the boat when you rented it?"

"No."

"They were there when the boat was returned?"

"Yes."

"Where is this boat now?" Hamilton Burger asked.

"In the possession of the police."

"When was it taken by the police?"

"About ten days later."

"You mean the sixteenth of June?"

"I believe it was the fifteenth."

"Did you find anything else in the boat, Mr. Gilly?"

"Yes, sir."

"What?"

"A sheath knife with the name 'Duane' engraved on the hilt on one side and the initials 'M.J.' on the other side."

"Where is that knife?"

"The police took it."

"When?"

"At the time they took the boat."

"Would you know that knife if you saw it again?"

"Yes."

Hamilton Burger unwrapped some tissue paper, produced a keen-bladed hunting knife, took it to the witness. "Have you ever seen this knife before?"

"Yes. That's the knife I found in the boat."

"Is it now in the same condition it was then?"

"No, sir. It was blood—I mean, it was stained with something red then, more than it is now."

"Yes, yes, some of those stains were removed at the crime laboratory for analysis," Hamilton Burger said suavely. "You may cross-examine the witness, Mr. Mason. And I now ask the clerk to mark this knife for indentification."

Mason smiled at Gilly. "Ever been convicted of a felony, Mr. Gilly?" Mason asked, his voice radiating good feeling.

Hamilton Burger jumped to his feet, apparently preparing to make an objection, then slowly settled back in his chair.

Gilly shifted his watery eyes from Mason's face to the floor.

"Yes, sir."

"How many times?" Mason asked.

"Twice."

"For what?"

"Once for larceny."

"And what was it for the second time?" Mason asked.

"Perjury," Gilly said.

Mason's smile was affable. "How far were you from the boat when you were watching it through your binoculars?"

"About . . . oh, a couple of good city blocks."

"How was the light?"

"It was just after daylight."

"There was fog?"

"Not fog. A sort of mist."

"A cold mist?"

"Yes. It was chilly."

"What did you use to wipe off the lenses of the binoculars—or did you wipe them?"

"I don't think I wiped them."

"And you saw one of these men fishing?"

"Yes, sir. The defendant held the fishing rod."

"And apparently he caught something?"

"A big body caught hold of the line."

"Have you seen people catch big fish before?"

"Yes, sir."

"And someimes when they have caught sharks you have seen them cut the sharks loose from the line or stab them to death before taking them off the hook?"

"This wasn't a shark."

"I'm asking you a question," Mason said. "Have you seen that?"

"Yes."

"Now, did this thing that was on the fishing line ever come entirely out of the water?"

"No, sir."

"Enough out of the water so you could see what it was?"

"It was almost all underwater all the time."

"You had never seen this man who rented the boat from you before he showed up to rent the boat?"

"No, sir."

"And you never saw him again?"

"No, sir."

"Do you know this knife wasn't in the boat when you rented it?"

"Yes."

"When did you first see it?"

"The afternoon of the sixth of June."

"Where?"

"In my boat."

"You had not noticed it before?"

"No."

"Yet you had looked in the boat?"

"Yes."

"And from the time the boat was returned to you until you found the knife, that boat was where anyone could have approached and dropped this knife into it, or tossed it to the bottom of the boat?"

"Well, I guess so. Anyone could have if he'd been snooping around down there."

"And how much rental did this mysterious man give you for the boat?"

"That's objected to as incompetent, irrelevant, and immaterial and not proper cross-examination," Hamilton Burger said.

"Well," Mason said, smiling, "I'll get at it in another way. Do you have an established rental rate for that boat, Mr. Gilly?"

"Yes, sir."

"How much is it?"

"A dollar to a dollar and a half an hour."

"Now then, did this stranger pay you the regular rental rate for the boat?"

"We made a special deal."

"You got *more* than your regular rental rate?"

"Yes, sir."

"How much more?"

"Objected to as not proper cross-examination, calling for facts not in evidence, and incompetent, irrelevant, and immaterial," Hamilton Burger said.

"Overruled," Judge Hartley said.

"How much rental?" Mason asked.

"I can't recall offhand. I think it was fifty dollars," Gilly said, his eyes refusing to meet those of Mason.

"Was that the figure that you asked, or the figure that the man offered?"

"The figure that I asked."

"Are you sure it was fifty dollars?"

"I can't remember too well. He gave me a bonus. I can't recall how much it was."

"Was it more than fifty dollars?"

"It could have been. I didn't count it. I just took the bills he gave me and put them in the locked box where I keep my money."

"You keep your money in the form of cash?"

"Some of it."

"Did you ever count this bonus?"

"I can't remember doing so."

"It could have been more than fifty dollars."

"I guess so. I don't know."

"Could it have been as much as a thousand dollars?"

"Oh, that's absurd!" Hamilton Burger protested to the Court.

"Overruled," Judge Hartley snapped.

"Was it?" Mason asked.

"I don't know."

"Did you enter it on your books?"

"I don't keep books."

"You don't know then how much cash is in this locked box where you keep your money?"

"Not to the penny."

"To the dollar?"

"No."

"To the hundred dollars?"

"No."

"Have you more than five hundred dollars in that box right now?"

"I don't know."

"More than five thousand dollars?"

"I can't tell."

"You may have?"

"Yes."

"Now, when were you convicted of perjury," Mason asked, "was that your first offense or second?"

"The second."

Mason smiled. "That's all, Mr. Gilly."

Judge Hartley glanced at the clock. "It appears that it is now time for the noon adjournment. Court will recess until two o'clock. During this time the jurors will not form or express any opinion as to the merits of the case, but will wait until the case is finally submitted before doing so. Nor will the jurors discuss the case among themselves or permit it to be discussed in their presence. The defendant is remanded to custody. Court will recess until two o'clock."

Paul Drake and Della Street, who had been occupying seats which had been reserved for them in the front of the courtroom, came toward Perry Mason.

Mason caught Paul Drake's eye, motioned them back. He turned to his client. "By the way," Mason said, "where *were* you on the night of the fifth and the morning of the sixth of June?"

"In my apartment, in bed and asleep."

"Can you prove it?" Mason asked.

Jefferson said scornfully, "Don't be absurd! I am unmarried, Mr. Mason. I sleep alone. There was no occasion for me to try and show where I was at that time, and there is none now. No one is going to pay any attention to the word of a perjurer and a crook who never saw me in his life before. Who is this scum of the waterfront? This whole thing is preposterous!"

"I'd be inclined to think so, too," Mason told him, "if it wasn't for that air of quiet confidence on the part of the district attorney. Therefore, it becomes very important for me to know exactly where you were on the night of the fifth and the morning of the sixth."

"Well," Jefferson said, "on the night of the fifth . . . that is, on the evening of the fifth I— I see no reason to go into that. On the sixth . . . from midnight on the fifth until eight-thirty on the morning of the sixth I was in my apartment. By nine o'clock on the morning of the sixth I was in my office, and I can *prove* where I was from a little after seven on the morning of the sixth."

"By whom?"

"By my associate, Walter Irving. He joined me for breakfast at seven in my apartment, and after that we went to the office."

"What about that knife?" Mason asked.

"It's mine. It was stolen from a suitcase in my apartment."

"Where did you get it?"

"It was a gift."

"From whom?"

"That has nothing to do with the case, Mr. Mason."

"Who gave it to you?"

"It's none of your business."

"I *have* to know who gave it to you, Jefferson."

"I am conducting my own affairs, Mr. Mason."

"I'm conducting your case."

"Go right ahead. Just don't ask me questions about women, that's all. I don't discuss my female friends with anyone."

"Is there anything you're ashamed of in connection with that gift?"

"Certainly not."

"Then tell me who gave it to you."

"It would be embarrassing to discuss any woman with you, Mr. Mason. That might bring about a situation where you'd feel I was perjuring myself about my relationship with women . . . when I get on the stand and answer questions put by the district attorney."

Mason studied Jefferson's face carefully. "Look here," he said. "Lots of times a weak case on the part of the prosecution is bolstered because the defendant breaks down under cross-examination. Now, I hope this case is never going to reach a point where it will become necessary to put on any defense. But if it does, I've got to be *certain* you're not lying to me."

Jefferson looked at Mason coldly. "I *never* lie to *anyone*," he said, and then turning away from Mason signaled to the officer that he was ready to be taken back to jail.

Della Street and Paul Drake fell in step with Mason as the lawyer started down the aisle.

"What do you make of it?" Mason asked.

"There sure is something fishy about this whole thing," Drake said. "It stinks. It has all the earmarks of a frame-up. How can Burger think people of that sort can put across a deal like this on a man like Duane Jefferson?"

"That," Mason said, "is the thing we're going to have to find out. Anything new?"

"Walter Irving's back."

"The deuce he is! Where has he been?"

"No one knows. He showed up about ten-thirty this morning. He was in court."

"Where?"

"Sitting in a back row, taking everything in."

Mason said, "There's something here that is completely and thoroughly contradictory. The whole case is cock-eyed."

"The police have something up their sleeves," Drake said. "They have some terrific surprise. I can't find out what it is. Do you notice that Hamilton Burger seems to remain thoroughly elated?"

"That's the thing that gets me," Mason said. "Burger puts on these witnesses and acts as though he's just laying a preliminary foundation. He doesn't seem to take too much interest in their stories, or whether I attack their characters or their credibility. He's playing along for something big."

"What about Irving?" Drake asked. "Are you going to be in touch with him?"

"Irving and I aren't on friendly terms. The last time he walked out of my office he was mad as a bucking bronco. He cabled his company, trying to get me fired. You haven't found out anything about Marline Chaumont or her brother?"

"I haven't found out where they are," Drake said, "but I think I've found out how they gave me the slip."

"How?" Mason asked. "I'm interested in that."

"It's so damn simple that it makes me mad I didn't get onto it sooner."

"What?"

Drake said, "Marline Chaumont simply took her suit-cases and had a porter deposit them in storage lockers. Then she took her brother out to an airport limousine, as though they were *incoming* passengers. She gave a porter the keys for two of the lockers, so two suitcases were brought out. She went in the limousine to a downtown hotel. She and her brother got out and completely vanished."

"Then, of course, she went back and got the other suitcases?" Mason asked.

"Presumably," Drake said, "she got a taxicab after she had her brother safely put away, went out to the airport, picked up the other two suitcases out of the storage lockers, and then rejoined her brother."

Mason said, "We've got to find her, Paul."

"I'm trying, Perry."

"Can't you check hotel registrations? Can't you—?"

"Look, Perry," Drake said, "I've checked every hotel registration that was made at about that time. I've checked with rental agencies for houses that were rented. I've checked with the utilities for connections that were put in at about that time. I've done everything I can think of. I've had girls telephoning the apartment houses to see if anyone made application for apartments. I've even checked the motels to see who registered on that date. I've done everything I can think of."

Mason paused thoughtfully. "Have you checked the car rental agencies, Paul?"

"What do you mean?"

"I mean the drive-yourself automobiles where a person rents an automobile, drives it himself, pays so much a day and so much a mile?"

The expression on Drake's face showed mixed emotions. "She wouldn't— Gosh, no! Good Lord, Perry! Maybe I overlooked a bet!"

Mason said, "Why couldn't she get a drive-yourself automobile, put her stuff in it, go to one of the outlying cities, rent a house there, then drive back with the automobile and—"

"I'd say it was one chance in ten thousand," Drake said, "but I'm not going to overlook it. It's all that's left."

"Okay," Mason said. "Try checking that idea for size, Paul."

Chapter 15

Promptly at two o'clock Court reconvened and Judge Hartley said, "Call your next witness, Mr. District Attorney."

Hamilton Burger hesitated a moment, then said, "I will call Mae Wallis Jordan."

Mae Jordan, quiet, demure, taking slow, steady steps, as though steeling herself to a task which she had long anticipated with extreme distaste, walked to the witness stand, was sworn, gave her name and address to the court reporter, and seated herself.

Hamilton Burger's voice fairly dripped sympathy. "You are acquainted with the defendant, Duane Jefferson, Miss Jordan?" he asked.

"Yes, sir."

"When did you first get acquainted with him?"

"Do you mean, when did I first see him?"

"When did you first get in touch with him," Hamilton Burger asked, "and how?"

"I first saw him after he came to the city here, but I have been corresponding with him for some time."

"When was the date that you first *saw* him? Do you know?"

"I know very well. He arrived by train. I was there to meet the train."

"On what date?"

"May seventeenth."

"Of this year?"

"Yes, sir."

"Now then, you had had some previous correspondence with the defendant?"

"Yes."

116

"How had that correspondence started?"

"It started as a . . . as a joke. As a gag."

"In what way?"

"I am interested in photography. In a photographic magazine there was an offer to exchange colored stereo photographs of Africa for stereo photographs of the south-western desert. I was interested and wrote to the box number in question."

"In South Africa?"

"Well, it was in care of the magazine, but it turned out that the magazine forwarded the mail to the person who had placed the ad in the magazine. That person was—"

"Just a moment," Mason interrupted. "We object to the witness testifying as to her conclusion. *She* doesn't know who put the ad in the magazine. Only the records of the magazine can show that."

"We will show them," Hamilton Burger said cheerfuly. "However, Miss Jordan, we'll just skip that at the moment. What happened?"

"Well, I entered into correspondence with the defendant."

"What was the nature of that correspondence generally?" Hamilton Burger asked. And then, turning to Mason, said, "Of course, I can understand that this may be objected to as not being the best evidence, but I am trying to expedite matters."

Mason, smiling, said, "I am always suspicious of one who tries to expedite matters by introducing secondary evidence. The letters themselves would be the best evidence."

"I only want to show the *general* nature of the correspondence," Hamilton Burger said.

"Objected to as not being the best evidence," Mason said, "and that the question calls for a conclusion of the witness."

"Sustained," Judge Hartley said.

"You received letters from South Africa?" Hamilton Burger asked, his voice showing a slight amount of irritation.

"Yes."

"Those letters were signed how?"

"Well . . . in various ways."

"What's that?" Hamilton Burger asked, startled. "I thought that—"

"Never mind what the district attorney thought," Mason said. "Let's have the *facts*."

"How were those letters signed?" Hamilton Burger asked.

"Some of them were signed with the name of the defendant, the first ones were."

"And where are those letters now?"

"They are gone."

"Where?"

"I destroyed them."

"Describe the contents of those letters," Hamilton Burger said unctuously. "Having proved, Your Honor, that the best evidence is no longer available, I am seeking to show by secondary evidence—"

"There are no objections," Judge Hartley said.

"I was going to state," Mason said, "that I would like to ask some questions on cross-examination as to the nature and contents of the letters and the time and manner of their destruction, in order to see whether I wished to object."

"Make you objection first, and then you may ask the questions," Judge Hartley said.

"I object, Your Honor, on the ground that no proper foundation for the introduction of secondary testimony has been laid and on the further ground that it now appears that at least some of these letters did not even bear the name of the defendant. In connection with that objection, I would like to ask a few questions."

"Go ahead," Hamilton Burger invited, smiling slightly.

Mason said, "You said that those letters were signed in various ways. What did you mean by that?"

"Well—" she said, and hesitated.

"Go on," Mason said.

"Well," she said, "some of the letters were signed with various . . . well, gag names."

"Such as what?" Mason asked.

"Daddy Longlegs was one," she said.

There was a ripple of mirth in the courtroom, which subsided as Judge Hartley frowned.

"And others?"

"Various names. You see we . . . we exchanged photographs . . . gag pictures."

"What do you mean by gag pictures?" Mason asked.

"Well, I am a camera fan, and the defendant is, too, and . . . we started corresponding formally at first, and then the correspondence became more personal. I . . . he asked me for a picture, and I . . . for a joke I—"

"Go ahead," Mason said. "What did you do?"

"I had taken a photograph of a very trim spinster who was no longer young, a rather interesting face, however, because it showed a great deal of character. I had a photograph of myself in a bathing suit and I . . . I made a trick enlargement, so that the face of the trim spinster was put on my body, and I sent it to him. I thought that if he was simply being flirtatious, that would stop him."

"Was it a joke, or was it intended to deceive him?" Mason asked.

She flushed and said, "That first picture was intended to deceive him. It was done so cunningly that it would be impossible for him to know that it was a composite picture—at least, I thought it would be impossible."

"And you asked him to send you a picture in return?"

"I did."

"And did you receive a picture?"

"Yes."

"What was it?"

"It was the face of a giraffe wearing glasses, grafted on the photograph of a huge figure of a heavily muscled man. Evidently, the figure of a wrestler or a weightlifter."

"And in that way," Mason asked, "you knew that he had realized your picture was a composite?"

"Yes."

"And what happened after that?"

"We exchanged various gag pictures. Each one trying to be a little more extreme than the other."

"And the letters?" Mason asked.

"The letters were signed with various names which would sort of fit in with the type of photograph."

"You so signed your letters to him?"

"Yes."

"And he so signed his letters to you?"

"Yes."

Mason made his voice elaborately casual. "He would sign letters to you, I suppose, as 'Your Prince,' or 'Sir Galahad,' or something like that?"

"Yes."

"Prince Charming?"

She gave a quick start. "Yes," she said. "As a matter of fact, at the last he signed *all* of his letters 'Prince Charming.'"

"Where are those letters now?" Mason asked.

"I destroyed his letters."

"And where are the letters that you wrote to him, if you know?"

"I . . . I destroyed them."

Hamilton Burger grinned. "Go right ahead, Mr. Mason. You're doing fine."

"How did you get ahold of them?" Mason asked.

"I . . . I went to his office."

"While he was there?" Mason asked.

"I—When I got the letters, he was there, yes."

Mason smiled at the district attorney. "Oh, I think, Your Honor, I have pursued this line of inquiry far enough. I will relinquish the right to any further questioning on the subject of the letters. I insist upon my objection, however. The witness can't swear that these letters ever came from this defendant. They were signed 'Prince Charming' and other names she said were gag names. That's her conclusion."

Judge Hartley turned toward the witness. "These letters were in response to letters mailed by you?"

"Yes, Your Honor."

"And how did you address the letters you mailed?"

"To 'Duane Jefferson, care of the South African Gem Importing and Exploration Company.'"

"At its South African address?"

"Yes, Your Honor."

"You deposited those letters in regular mail channels?"

"Yes, Your Honor."

"And received these letters in reply?"

"Yes, Your Honor."

"The letters showed they were in reply to those mailed by you?"

"Yes, Your Honor."

"And you burned them?"

"Yes, Your Honor."

"The objection is overruled," Judge Hartley said. "You may introduce secondary evidence of their contents, Mr. District Attorney."

Hamilton Burger bowed slightly, turned to the witness. "Tell us what was in those letters which were destroyed," he said.

"Well, the defendant adopted the position that he was lonely and far from the people he knew, that he didn't have any girl friends, and . . . oh, it was all a gag. It's *so* difficult to explain."

"Go ahead; do the best you can," Hamilton Burger said.

"We adopted the attitude of . . . well, we pretended it was a lonely hearts correspondence. He would write and tell me how very wealthy and virtuous he was and what a good husband he would make, and I would write and tell him how beautiful I was and how—Oh, it's just simply out of the question to try and explain it in cold blood this way!"

"Out of context, so to speak?" Hamilton Burger asked.

"Yes," she said. "That's just it. You have to understand the mood and the background, otherwise you wouldn't be able to get the picture at all. The letters, standing by themselves, would appear to be hopelessly foolish, utterly asinine. That was why I felt I had to have them back in my possession."

"Go ahead," Hamilton Burger said. "What did you do?"

"Well, finally Duane Jefferson wrote me one serious letter. He told me that his company had decided to open a branch office in the United States, that it was to be located here, and that he was to be in charge of it and that he was looking forward to seeing me."

"And what did you do?"

"All of a sudden I was in a terrific panic. It was one thing to carry on a joking correspondence with a man who was thousands of miles away and quite another thing suddenly to meet that man face to face. I was flustered and embarrassed."

"Go on. What did you do?"

"Well, of course, when he arrived—he wired me what train he was coming on, and I was there to meet him and— that was when things began to go wrong."

"In what way?"

"He gave me a sort of brush-off, and *he* wasn't the type of person *I* had anticipated. Of course," she went on hastily, "I know what a little fool I was to get a preconceived notion of a man I'd never seen, but I had built up a very great regard for him. I considered him as a friend and I was terribly disappointed."

"Then what?" Hamilton Burger asked.

"Then I called two or three times on the telephone and talked with him, and I went out with him one night."

"And what happened?"

She all but shuddered. "The man was utterly impossible," she said, glaring down at the defendant. "He was patronizing in a cheap, tawdry way. His manner showed that he had completely mistaken the tone of my correspondence. He regarded me as . . . he treated me as if I were a . . . he showed no respect, no consideration. He had none of the finer feelings."

"And what did *you* do?"

"I told him I wanted my letters back."

"And what did he do?"

She glared at Duane Jefferson. "He told me I could *buy* them back."

"So what did you do?"

"I determined to get those letters back. They were mine, anyway."

"So what did you do?"

"On June fourteenth I went to the office at a time when I knew neither the defendant nor Mr. Irving would normally be there."

"And what did you do?" Hamilton Burger asked.

"I entered the office."

"For what purpose?"

"For the sole purpose of finding the letters I had written."

"You had reason to believe those letters were in the office?"

"Yes. He told me they were in his desk and that I could come and get them at any time after I had complied with his terms."

"What happened?"

"I couldn't find the letters. I looked and I looked, and I pulled open the drawers of the desk and then—"

"Go on," Hamilton Burger said.

"And the door opened," she said.

"And who was in the doorway?"

"The defendant, Duane Jefferson."

"Alone?"

"No. His associate, Walter Irving, was with him."

"What happened?"

"The defendant used vile language. He called me names that I have never been called before."

"And then what?"

"He made a grab for me and—"

"And what did you do?"

"I backed up and tipped over a chair and fell over. Then Mr. Irving grabbed my ankles and held me. The defendant accused me of snooping and I told him I was there only to get my letters."

"Then what?"

"Then he stood for a moment looking at me in apparent

surprise, and then said to Mr. Irving, 'Damned if I don't believe she's right!' "

"Then what?"

"Then the phone rang and Irving picked up the receiver, listened for a minute and said, 'Good God! The police!' "

"Go on," Hamilton Burger said.

"So the defendant ran over to a filing cabinet, jerked it open, pulled out a whole package of my letters tied up with string and said, 'Here, you little fool! Here are your letters. Take them and get out! The police are looking for you. Someone saw you break into the place, and the police have been notified. Now, see what a damn fool you are!'"

"What happened?"

"He started pushing me toward the door. Then Mr. Irving pushed something into my hand and said, 'Here, take these. They'll be a reward for keeping your big mouth shut.' "

"And what did you do?"

"As soon as they pushed me out of the door, I made a dash for the women's restroom."

"Go on," Hamilton Burger said.

"And just as I opened the door of the restroom, I saw the defendant and Walter Irving run out of their office and dash to the men's room."

"Then what?"

"I didn't wait to see any more. I dashed into the restroom and unfastened the string on the package of letters I had been given, looked through the contents to see that they were mine, and destroyed them."

"How did you destroy them?"

"I put them in the wastepaper receptacle with the used towels, where they would be picked up and incinerated."

"And then what did you do?"

"Then," she said, "I was trapped. I knew the police were coming. I—"

"Go ahead," Hamilton Burger said.

"I had to do something to get out of there."

"And *what* did you do?" Hamilton Burger said, a smile on his face.

"I felt that perhaps the exits might be watched, that I must have been seen by someone who had given the police a good description, so I . . . I looked around for someplace to go, and I saw a door which had the sign on it saying, 'Perry Mason, Attorney at Law, Enter.' I'd heard of Perry Mason, of course, and I thought perhaps I could hand him a line, telling him I wanted a divorce or something of that sort, or that I'd been in an automobile accident . . . just make up a good story, anything to hold his interest. That would enable me to be in his office when the police arrived. I felt I could hold his interest long enough to avoid the police. I wanted to stay there just long enough so I could get out after the police had given up the search. I realize now that it was a crazy idea, but it was the only available avenue of escape. As it happened, Fate played into my hands."

"In what way?"

"It seemed Mr. Mason's secretaries were expecting a typist. They'd telephoned some agency and a typist was supposed to be on her way up. I stood, hesitating, in the doorway for a moment, and the receptionist took me for the typist. She asked me if I was the typist, so of course I told her yes and went to work."

"And," Hamilton Burger said smugly, "you worked in the office of Perry Mason that afternoon?"

"I worked there for some little time, yes."

"And then what?"

"When the coast was clear I made my escape."

"When was that?"

"Well, I was working on a document. I was afraid that if it was finished, Mr. Mason would ring up the secretarial agency to find out what the bill was. I just didn't know what to do. So when there was a good break, I slipped down to the restroom, then to the elevator and went home."

"You have mentioned something that was pushed into your hand. Do you know what that consisted of?"

"Yes."

"What?"

"Diamonds. Two diamonds."

"When did you find out about them?"

"After I'd been working for a few minutes. I'd slipped what had been given me into my handbag. So when I had a good chance I looked. I found two small packets of tissue paper. I removed the paper and found two diamonds.

"I got in a panic. I suddenly realized that if these men should claim the intruder had stolen diamonds from their office, I'd be framed. I wouldn't have any possible defense anyone would believe. So I just had to get rid of these diamonds. I realized right away I'd walked into a trap."

"What did you do?"

"I stuck the diamonds to the underside of the desk, where I was working in Mr. Mason's office."

"How did you stick them to this desk?"

"With chewing gum."

"How much chewing gum?"

"A perfectly terrific amount. I had about twelve sticks in my purse, and I chewed them all up and got a big wad of gum. Then I put the diamonds in the gum and pushed them up against the underside of the desk."

"Where are those diamonds now?"

"As far as *I* know, they're still there."

"Your Honor," Hamilton Burger said, "if the Court please, I suggest that an officer of this court be dispatched to the office of Perry Mason, with instructions to look at the place described by this witness and bring back the wad of chewing gum containing those two diamonds."

Judge Hartley looked at Mason questioningly.

Mason smiled at the judge. "*I* certainly would have no objection, Your Honor."

"Very well," Judge Hartley ruled. "It will be the order of the Court that an officer of this court proceed to take those diamonds and impound them."

"And may they be sent for *immediately,* Your Honor," Hamilton Burger asked, "before . . . well, before something happens to them?"

"And what would happen to them?" Judge Hartley asked.

"Well, now that it is known," Hamilton Burger said, "now that the testimony has come out . . . I . . . well, I would dislike to have anything happen to the evidence."

"So would I," Mason said heartily. "I join the prosecutor's request. I suggest that one of the deputy district attorneys instruct an officer to proceed at once to my office."

"Can you designate the desk that was used by this young lady?" Hamilton Burger asked.

"The desk in question was one that was placed in the law library. It can be found there."

"Very well," the judge ruled. "You may take care of that matter, Mr. District Attorney. Now, go on with your questioning."

Hamilton Burger walked over to the clerk's desk, picked up the knife which had been marked for identification. "I show you a dagger with an eight-inch blade, one side of the hilt being engraved with the word 'Duane,' the other side with the initials 'M.J.' I will ask you if you are familiar with that knife."

"I am. It is a knife which I sent the defendant at his South African address as a Christmas present last Christmas. I told him he could use it to protect . . . protect my honor."

The witness began to cry.

"I think," Hamilton Burger said suavely, "that those are all of the questions I have of this witness. You may cross-examine, Mr. Mason."

Mason waited patiently until Mae Jordan had dried her eyes and looked up at him. "You are, I believe, a very fast and accurate typist?"

"I try to be competent."

"And you worked in my office on the afternoon in question?"

"Yes."

"Do you know anything about gems?"

"Not particularly."

"Do you know the difference between a real diamond and an imitation diamond?"

"It didn't take an expert to tell those stones. Those were very high-grade stones. I recognized what they were as soon as I saw them."

"Had you bought those stones from the defendant?" Mason asked.

"What do you mean, had I bought those stones?"

"Did you pay him anything? Give him any consideration?"

"Certainly not," she snapped.

"Did you pay Mr. Irving for those stones?"

"No."

"Then you knew those stones did not belong to you?" Mason asked.

"They were given to me."

"Oh, then you thought they were yours?"

"I felt certain I'd walked into a trap. I felt those men would say I'd gone to their office and stolen those diamonds. It would be my word against theirs. I knew they hadn't given me two very valuable diamonds just to keep quiet about having exchanged letters."

"You say *they* gave you the diamonds. Did you receive them from Jefferson or from Irving?"

"From Mr. Irving."

Mason studied the defiant witness for a moment. "You started corresponding with the defendant while he was in South Africa?"

"Yes."

"And wrote him love letters?"

"They were not love letters."

"Did they contain matters which you wouldn't want this jury to see?"

"They were foolish letters, Mr. Mason. Please don't try to put anything in them that wasn't in them."

"I am asking you," Mason said, "as to the nature of the letters."

"They were *very foolish* letters."

"Would you say they were indiscreet?"

"I would say they were indiscreet."

"You wanted them back?"

"I felt . . . well . . . foolish about the whole thing."

"So you wanted the letters back?"

"Yes, very badly."

"And, in order to get them back, you were willing to commit a crime?"

"I wanted the letters back."

"Please answer the question. You were willing to commit a crime in order to get the letters back?"

"I don't know that it's a crime to enter an office to get things that belong to me."

"Did you believe it was illegal to use a skelton key to enter property belonging to another person, so that you could take certain things?"

"I was trying to get possession of property that belonged to me."

"Did you believe that it was illegal to use a skelton key to open that door?"

"I . . . I didn't consult a lawyer to find out about my rights."

"Where did you get the key which opened the door?"

"I haven't said I had a key."

"You've admitted you entered the office at a time when you knew both Jefferson and Irving would not be there."

"What if I did? I went to get my own property."

"If you had a key which opened the door of that office, where did you get it?"

"Where does one ordinarily get keys?"

"From a locksmith?"

"Perhaps."

"Did you get a key to that office from a locksmith?"

"I will answer no questions about keys."

"And suppose the Court should instruct you that you had to answer such questions?"

"I would refuse on the grounds that any testimony from me relating to the manner in which I entered that office would tend to incriminate me, and therefore I would not have to answer the question."

"I see," Mason said. "But you have already admitted that you entered the office illegally. Therefore, an attempt to exercise your constitutional prerogative would be too late."

"Now, if the Court please," Hamilton Burger said, "I would like to be heard on this point. I have given this question very careful thought. The Court will note that the witness simply stated that she entered the office at a time when the defendant and his associate were absent. She has not stated *how* she entered the office. As far as her testimony is concerned, the door could well have been unlocked; and, inasmuch as this is a public office, where it is expected the public will enter in order to transact business, there would have been nothing illegal about an entrance made in the event the door had been unlocked. Therefore, the witness is in a position, if she so desires, to refuse to testify as to the manner in which she entered that office, on the ground that it might tend to incriminate her."

Judge Hartley frowned. "That's rather an unusual position for a witness called on behalf of the prosecution, Mr. District Attorney."

"It's an unusual case, Your Honor."

"Do you wish to be heard on that point, Mr. Mason?" Judge Hartley asked.

Mason smiled and said, "I would like to ask the witness a few more questions."

"I object to any more cross-examination on this point," Hamilton Burger said, his voice showing exasperation and a trace of apprehension. "The witness has made her position plain. Counsel doesn't dare to cross-examine her about the pertinent facts in the case, so he continually harps upon the one point where this young woman, yielding to her emotions, has put herself in an embarrassing position. He keeps prolonging this moment, as a cat plays with a mouse, hoping thereby to prejudice the jury against this witness. The witness has made her position plain. She refuses to answer questions on this phase of the matter."

Mason smiled. "I have been accused of prolonging this phase of the examination in an attempt to prejudice the jury.

I don't want to prejudice the jury. I'd like to get information which the jurors want.

"When the district attorney was prolonging the examination of Mr. Gilly in an attempt to prejudice the jury against the defendant, you didn't hear me screaming. What's sauce for the goose should be sauce for the gander."

Judge Hartley smiled. "The objection is overruled. Go ahead with your questions."

"Will you tell us the name of the person who furnished you with the key that enabled you to get into the office of the South African Gem Importing and Exploration Company?"

"No."

"Why not?"

"Because, if I answered that question, it would tend to incriminate me, and therefore I shall refuse to answer."

"You have discussed this phase of your testimony with the district attorney?"

"Oh, Your Honor," Hamilton Burger said, "this is the same old gambit so frequently pursued by defense attorneys. I will stipulate that this witness has discussed her testimony with me. I would not have put her on the stand unless I knew that her testimony would be pertinent and relevant. The only way I could know what it was, was to talk with her."

Mason kept his eyes on the witness. "You have discussed this phase of your testimony with the district attorney?"

"Yes."

"And have discussed with him what would happen in case you were asked a question concerning the name of the person who furnished you the keys?"

"Yes."

"And told him you would refuse to testify on the ground that it would incriminate you?"

"Yes."

"Did you make that statement to the district attorney, or did he suggest to you that you could refuse to answer the question on that ground?"

"Well, I . . . I . . . of course I know my rights."

"But you have just stated," Mason said, "that you didn't know that it was a crime for you to enter an office to get property that belonged to you."

"Well, I . . . I think there's a nice legal point there. As I now understand it, a public office . . . that is, a place that is intended to be open to the public is different from a private residence. And where property belongs to me—"

Mason smiled. "Then you are *now* taking the position, Miss Jordan, that it was no crime for you to enter that office?"

"No."

"Oh, you are *now* taking the position that it *was* a crime for you to enter that office?"

"I now understand that under the circumstances it—I refuse to answer that question on the ground that the answer may incriminate me."

"In other words, the district attorney suggested to you that you should consider it was a crime, and therefore you could refuse to answer certain questions when I asked them?"

"We discussed it."

"And the suggestion came from the district attorney that it would be well under the circumstances for you to refuse to answer certain questions which I might ask on cross-examination. Is that right?"

"There were certain questions I told him I wouldn't answer."

"And he suggested that you could avoid answering them by claiming immunity on the ground that you couldn't be forced to incriminate yourself?"

"Well, in a way, yes."

"Now then," Mason said, "you had two diamonds with you when you left that office?"

"Yes."

"They didn't belong to you?"

"They were given to me."

"By whom?"

"By Mr. Irving, who told me to take them."

"Did he say *why* you were to take them?"

"He said to take them and keep my big mouth shut."

"And you took them?"

"Yes."

"And you kept your mouth shut?"

"I don't know what you mean by that."

"You didn't tell anyone about the diamonds?"

"Not at that time."

"You knew they were valuable?"

"I'm not simple, Mr. Mason."

"Exactly," Mason said. "You knew they were diamonds and you knew they were valuable?"

"Certainly."

"And you took them?"

"Yes."

"And what did you do with them?"

"I've told you what I did with them. I fastened them to the underside of the desk in your office."

"Why?" Mason asked.

"Because I wanted a place to keep them."

"You could have put them in your purse. You could have put them in your pocket," Mason said.

"I . . . I didn't want to. I didn't want to have to explain how I came by the diamonds."

"To whom?"

"To anybody who might question me."

"To the police?"

"To *anyone* who might question me, Mr. Mason. I felt I had walked into a trap and that I was going to be accused of having stolen two diamonds."

"But you had been given those diamonds?"

"Yes, but I didn't think anyone would believe me when I told them so."

"Then you don't expect the jury to believe your story now?"

"Objected to," Hamilton Burger snapped. "Argumentative."

"Sustained," Judge Hartley said.

"Isn't it a fact," Mason asked, "that someone who gave you a key to the office which you entered illegally and unlawfully, also gave you a package of diamonds which you were to plant in that office in a place where they would subsequently be found by the police?"

"No!"

"Isn't it a fact that you carried those diamonds into the building wrapped up in tissue paper, that you put those diamonds in a package and concealed them in the office, that you were forced to leave hurriedly because you learned the police had been tipped off, and after you got in my office and started to work, you checked through your purse in order to make certain that you had disposed of all of the diamonds and to your horror found that two of the diamonds you were supposed to have planted in that office had been left in your purse, and that, therefore, in a panic, you tried to get rid of of those diamonds by the means you have described?"

"Just a moment!" Hamilton Burger shouted. "I object to this on the ground that it assumes facts not in evidence, that it is not proper cross-examination, that there is no foundation for the assumption that—"

"The objection is overruled," Judge Hartley snapped.

"Isn't it a fact," Mason asked, "that you did what I have just outlined?"

"Absolutely not. I took no diamonds with me when I went to that office. I had no diamonds in my possession when I went in."

"But you don't dare to tell us who gave you a key to that office?"

"I refuse to answer questions about that."

"Thank you," Mason said. "I have no further questions."

Mae Jordan left the stand. The jurors watched her with some skepticism.

Hamilton Burger called other witnesses who established technical background—the exact position of the cruise ship in the harbor when Baxter jumped overboard, passengers who had seen Baxter jump and the owner of a launch which had been cruising in the vicinity. He also introduced police experts who had examined the bloodstains on Gilly's boat and bloodstains on the knife and pronounced them to be human blood.

Mason had no cross-examination except for the expert who had examined the bloodstains.

"*When* did you make your examination?" Mason asked.

"June nineteenth."

"At a time when the bloodstains were at least ten days to two weeks old?"

"So I should judge."

"On the boat?"

"Yes."

"On the knife?"

"Yes."

"They could have been older?"

"Yes."

"They could have been a month old?"

"Well, they could have been."

"The only way you have of knowing when those bloodstains got on the boat was from a statement made to you by Jack Gilly?"

"Yes."

"And did you know Jack Gilly had previously been convicted of perjury?"

The witness squirmed.

"Objected to as incompetent, irrelevant, and immaterial and not proper cross-examination," Hamilton Burger said.

"Sustained," Judge Hartley snapped. "Counsel can confine his cross-examination to the bloodstains, the nature of the tests, and the professional competency of the witness."

"That's all," Mason said. "I have no more questions."

Max Dutton, Hamilton Burger's last witness of the afternoon, was distinctly a surprise witness. Dutton testified that he lived in Brussels; he had come by airplane to testify at the request of the district attorney. He was, he testified, an expert on gems. He used a system of making models of gems so that it would be possible to identify any particular stone of sufficient value to make it worth-while. He made microscopic measurements of the dimensions, of the angles, of the facets, and of the locations of any flaws. The witness testified he maintained permanent records of his identifications, which facilitated appraisals, insurance recoveries and the identification of stolen stones.

He had, he said, been employed by Munroe Baxter during his lifetime; Munroe Baxter had given him some gems and asked him to arrange for the identification of the larger stones, so that they could be readily identified if necessary.

The witness tried to state what Munroe Baxter had told him—the manner in which he had received the stones—but on objection by Perry Mason the objection was sustained by the Court. However, Hamilton Burger was able to show that the stones came to the witness in a box bearing the imprint of the Paris office of the South African Gem Importing and Exploration Company.

The witness testified that he had selected the larger stones and had made complete charts of those stones, so that they could be identified. He further stated that he had examined a package of stones which had been given him by the police and which he understood had been recovered from the desk of the defendant, and that ten of those stones had proved to be identical to the stones he had so carefully charted.

"Cross-examine," Hamilton Burger said.

"This system that you have worked out for identifying stones takes into consideration every possible identifying mark on the stones?" Mason asked.

"It does."

"It would, therefore, enable anyone to duplicate those stones, would it not?"

"No, sir, it would not. You might cut a stone to size; you might get the angle of the facets exactly the same. But the flaws in the stone would not be in the proper position with relation to the facets."

"It would, however, be possible to make a duplication in the event you could find a stone that had certain flaws?"

"That is very much like asking whether it would be possible to duplicate fingerprints, provided you could find a person who had exactly identical ridges and whorls," the witness said.

"Do you then wish to testify under oath that your system of identifying stones is as accurate as the identification of individuals through the science of fingerprinting?" Mason asked.

The witness hesitated a moment, then said, "Not quite."

"That's all," Mason announced, smiling. "No further questions."

The court took its evening adjournment.

As Mason gathered his papers together Walter Irving pushed his way through the crowd that was leaving the courtroom. He came up to Mason's table. His grin was somewhat sheepish.

"I guess perhaps I owe you an apology," he said.

"You don't owe me anything," Mason told him. "And make no mistake about it, I don't owe you anything."

"You don't owe me anything," Irving said, "but I'm going to make an apology anyway. And I'm further going to tell you that that Jordan girl is a brazen-faced liar. I *think* she broke into that office to plant those diamonds; but regardless of her purpose in getting into the office, there was never any scene such as she testified to. We didn't get back from lunch until after she had done what she wanted to do in that office and had skipped out. We can prove that, and that one fact makes that Jordan girl a damn liar.

"And what's more, I didn't give that Jordan girl any diamonds," Irving said. "I didn't tell her to keep her mouth shut. Now that I've seen her, I remember having seen her at the train. She met Duane and tried to force herself on him. As far as I know, that's the only time in my life I've ever set eyes on her. That girl is playing some deep game, and she's not playing it for herself, Mr. Mason. There's something behind it, something very sinister and something being engineered by powerful interests that have made a dupe of your district attorney."

"I hope so," Mason said. "Where have you been, incidentally?"

"I've been in Mexico. I admit, I underestimated your abilities, but I was trying to give you an opportunity to direct suspicion to me in case you wanted to."

"Well, I haven't wanted to," Mason said, and then added significantly, "yet."

Irving grinned at him. "That's the spirit, Counselor. You can always make a pass at me and confuse the issues as far as the jury is concerned, even if you don't want to be friendly with me. Remember that I'm available as a suspect."

Mason looked into his eyes. "Don't think I'll ever forget it."

Irving's grin was one of pure delight. His reddish-brown eyes met the cold, hard gaze of the lawyer with steady affability. "Now you're cooking with gas! Any time you want me, I'll be available, and I can, of course, give Duane a complete alibi for the morning of the sixth. We had breakfast together a little after seven, got to the office shortly before nine, and he was with me all morning."

"How about the evening of the fifth?" Mason asked.

Irving's eyes shifted.

"Well?" Mason asked.

"Duane was out somewhere."

"Where?"

"With some woman."

"Who?"

Irving shrugged his shoulders.

Mason said, "You can see what's happening here. If the district attorney makes enough of a case so that I have to put the defendant on the stand, there is every possibility that Duane Jefferson's manner, his aloofness, his refusal to answer certain questions, will prejudice his case with the jury."

"I know," Irving said. "I know exactly what you're up

against. Before you ever put him on the stand, Mr. Mason, let me talk with him and I'll hammer some sense into his head, even if it does result in his undying enmity forever afterwards. In short, I want you to know that you can count on me all the way through."

"Yes," Mason said, "I understand you sent a most co-operative cablegram to your company in South Africa?"

Irving kept grinning and his eyes remained steady. "That's right," he said. "I asked the company to fire you. I'm sending another one tonight, which will be a lot different. You haven't found Marline Chaumont yet, have you?"

"No," Mason admitted.

Irving lost his grin. "I told you you wouldn't. That's where you loused the case up, Mason. Aside from that, you're doing fine."

And, as though completely assured of Mason's goodwill, Walter Irving turned and sauntered out of the courtroom.

Chapter 16

Back in his office that evening, Mason paced the floor. "Hang it, Paul!" he said to the detective. "Why is Hamilton Burger so completely confident?"

"Well, you jarred him a couple of times this afternoon," Drake said. "He was so mad he was quivering like a bowl of jelly."

"I know he was mad, Paul. He was angry, he was irritated, he was annoyed, but he was still sure of himself.

"Hamilton Burger hates me. He'd love to get me out on a limb over a very deep pool and then saw off the limb. He wouldn't even mind if he got slightly wet from the resulting splash. Now, there's something in this case that we don't know about."

"Well," Drake said, "as far as this case is concerned, what does he have, Perry?"

"So far he doesn't have anything," Mason said. "That's what worries me. Why should he have that much assurance over a case which means nothing. He has a woman adventuress and a smuggler; he has a man who concededly planned to fake a suicide. The man was a strong swimmer. He had an air tank under his clothes. He did exactly what he had planned he was going to do, to wit, jump over the side of the ship and disappear, so that people would think he was dead.

"Then Hamilton Burger brings on the scum of the earth, the sweepings of the waterfront. He uses a man who deliberately rented a boat to be used in an illegal activity, a man who has been twice convicted of felony. His last conviction was for perjury. The jury isn't going to believe that man."

"And what about the girl?" Della Street asked.

"That's different," Mason said. "That girl made a good impression on the jury. Apparently, she was hired to take those gems to the office and plant them. The jury doesn't know that. Those jurors are taking her at face value."

"Figure value," Paul Drake corrected. "Why did you let her off so easy, Perry?"

"Because every time she answered a question she was getting closer to the jury. Those jurors like her, Paul. I'm going to ask to recall her for further cross-examination. When I do that, I want to have the lowdown on her. You're going to put out operatives who will dig up the dirt on her. I want to know everything about her, all about her past, her friends, and before I question her again, I want to know where she got that key which opened the office."

Drake merely nodded.

"Well," Mason said impatiently, "aren't you going to get busy, Paul?"

The detective sat grinning. "I am busy, Perry. I've been busy. This is once I read your mind. I knew what you'd want. The minute that girl got off the stand, I started a whole bunch of men working. I left this unlisted number of yours with my confidential secretary. She may call any minute with some hot stuff."

Mason smiled. "Give yourself a merit badge, Paul. Hang it, there's nothing that gets a lawyer down worse than having to cross-examine a demure girl who has hypnotized the jury. I can't keep shooting blind, Paul. The next time I start sniping at her, I've got to have ammunition that will score dead-center hits.

"Now, here's something else you'll have to do."

"What's that, Perry?"

"Find Munroe Baxter."

"You don't think he's dead?"

"I'm beginning to think Walter Irving was right. I think the supposedly half-witted brother of Marline Chaumont may well be Baxter, despite those hospital records. In a deal of this magnitude we may find a big loophole. If this fellow in the mental hospital was so much of a zombie, what was to prevent Marline Chaumont from identifying him as her brother, getting him out, then farming him out and substituting Munroe Baxter? What are we doing about finding her, Paul?"

"Well we're making headway, thanks to you," Drake said. "I'm kicking myself for being a stupid fool. You were right about those car rentals, and I sure overlooked a bet there. Two of those car rentals have agencies right there at the airport. In order to rent a car, you have to show your driving license. That means you have to give your right name."

"You mean Marline Chaumont rented a car under her own name?"

"That's right. Showed her driving license, rented the automobile and took it out."

"Her brother was with her?"

"Not at that time. She left the airport by limousine as an incoming passenger, went uptown with her brother and two suitcases, then came back, rented a car, picked up the other two suitcases, drove out, picked up her brother, and then went someplace."

"Where?" Mason asked.

"Now, that's something I wish I knew. However, we stand a chance of finding out. The car rental is predicated on the mileage driven, as well as on a per diem charge. The mileage indicator on the car when Marline Chaumont brought it back showed it had been driven sixty-two miles."

Mason thought a moment, then snapped his fingers.

"What now?" Drake asked.

"She went out to one of the suburban cities," Mason said. "She's rented a place in one of those suburbs. Now then, she'll want to rent another car, and again she'll have to use her driving license. She was afraid to keep that car she had rented at the airport because she thought we might be checking there."

"We would have been checking within a matter of hours if I'd been on my toes," Drake said ruefully.

"All right," Mason said, "she rented a car there. She was afraid we might trace her, get the license number of the car, have it posted as a hot car and pick her up. So she got rid of that car just as soon as she could. Then she went to one of the outlying towns where they have a car rental agency and signed up for another car. She's had to do it under her own name because of the license angle. Get your men busy, Paul, and cover *all* of the car rental agencies in those outlying towns."

Paul Drake wormed his way out of the chair to stand erect, stretch, say, "Gosh, I'm all in myself. I don't see how you stand a pace like this, Perry."

He went over, picked up the unlisted telephone, said, "Let me call my office and get people started on some of this."

Drake dialed the number, said, "Hello. This is Paul. I want a bunch of men put out to cover all of the outlying towns. I want to check every car rental agency for a car rented by Marline Chaumont . . . That's right. Everything.

"Now you can— How's that? . . . Wait a minute now," Drake said. "Give that to me slow. I want to make some notes. Who made the report? . . . All right, bring it down here at once. I'm in Mason's office—and get those men started."

Drake hung up the telephone and said, "We've got something, Perry."

"What?"

"We've found out the ace that Hamilton Burger is holding up his sleeve."

"You're sure?"

"Dead sure. One of the detectives who worked on the case knows the angle. He tipped a newspaper reporter off to come and see you get torn to ribbons tomorrow, and the reporter pumped him enough to find out what it was. That reporter is very friendly with one of my men, and we got a tip-off."

"What is it?" Mason asked.

"We'll have all the dope in a minute. They're bringing

143

the report down here," Drake said. "It concerns the woman that Duane Jefferson is trying to protect."

Mason said, "Now, we're getting somewhere, Paul. If I know that information, I don't care what Hamilton Burger things he's going to do with it. I'll out-general him somehow."

They waited anxiously until knuckles tapped on the door. Drake opened the door, took an envelope from his secretary, said, "You're getting operatives out checking those car rentals?"

"That's already being done, Mr. Drake. I put Davis in charge of it, and he's on the telephone right now."

"Fine," Drake said. "Let's take a look. I'll give you the dope, Perry."

Drake opened the envelope, pulled out the sheets of flimsy, looked through them hastily, then whistled.

"All right," Mason said, "give."

Drake said, "The night of June fifth Jefferson was down at a nightspot with a woman. It was the woman's car. The parking attendant parked the car and some customer scratched a fender. The attendant got records of license numbers and all that. The woman got in a panic, gave the parking attendant twenty bucks, and told him to forget the whole thing.

"Naturally, the attendant had the answer as soon as that happened. She was a married woman. There's no doubt the guy with her was Duane Jefferson."

"Who was she?" Mason asked.

"A woman by the name of Nan Ormsby."

"Okay," Mason said. "Perhaps I can use this. It'll depend on how far the affair has gone."

Drake, who had continued reading the report, suddenly gave another whistle.

"What now?" Mason asked.

"Hold everything," Drake said. "You have a juror number eleven Alonzo Martin Liggett?"

"What about him?" Mason asked.

"He's a close friend of Dan Ormsby. Ormsby is in

partnership with his wife. They have a place called 'Nan and Dan, Realtors.' Nan Ormsby has been having trouble with her husband. She wants a settlement. He doesn't want the kind of settlement she wants. He hasn't been able to get anything on her yet.

"Now, with a juror who is friendly to Dan Ormsby, you can see what'll happen."

"Good Lord!" Mason said. "If Hamilton Burger uses that lever—"

"Remember, this tip comes straight from Hamilton Burger's office," Drake said.

Mason sat in frowning concentration.

"How bad is it?" Drake asked.

"It's a perfect setup for a D.A.," Mason said. "If he can force me to put my client on the stand, he can to go town. The jury isn't going to like Duane Jefferson's pseudo-British manner, his snobbishness. You know how they feel about people who get tied up with the British and then become more English than the English, and that's what Jefferson has done. He's cultivated all those mannerisms. So Hamilton Burger will start boring into him—he was breaking up a home, he was out with a married woman—and there's Dan Ormsby's friend sitting on the jury."

"Any way you can beat that, Perry?" Drake asked.

"Two ways," Mason said, "and I don't like either one. I can either base all of my fight on trying to prove that there's been no *corpus delicti*, and keep the case from going to the jury, or, if the judge doesn't agree with me on that, I'll put the defendant on the stand, but confine my direct examination to where he was at five o'clock on the morning of the sixth and roar like the devil if the district attorney tries to examine him as to the night of the fifth. Since I wouldn't have asked him anything about the night of the fifth—only the morning of the sixth—I can claim the D.A. can't examine him as to anything on the night of the fifth."

"He'll make a general denial that he committed the crime?" Drake asked.

Mason nodded.

"Won't that open up the question of where he was on the night of the fifth when the boat was being rented?"

"The prosecution's case shows that the defendant wasn't seen until the morning of the sixth, after the boat had been rented—that is, that's the prosecution's case so far. We have the testimony of Jack Gilly to that effect."

"Well," Drake said, "I'll go down to my office and start things going. I'll have my men on the job working all night. You'd better get some sleep, Perry."

Mason's nod showed his preoccupation with other thoughts. "I've got to get this thing straight, Paul. I have a sixth sense that's warning me. I guess it's the way Hamilton Burger has been acting. This is one case where I've got to watch every time I put my foot down that I'm not stepping right in the middle of a trap."

"Well," Drake said, "you pace the floor and I'll cover the country, Perry. Between us, we may be in a better position tomorrow morning."

Mason said, "I should have known. Burger has been triumphant, yet his case is a matter of patchwork. It wasn't the strength of his own case that made him triumphant, but the weakness of my case."

"And now that you know, can you detour the pitfalls?" Drake asked.

"I can try," Mason said grimly.

Chapter 17

Judge Hartley called Court to order promptly at ten.

Hamilton Burger said, "I have a couple more questions to ask Mr. Max Dutton, the gem expert."

"Just a moment," Mason said. "If the Court please, I wish to make a motion. I feel that perhaps this motion should be made without the presence of the jury."

Judge Hartley frowned. "I am expecting a motion at the conclusion of the prosecution's case," he said. "Can you not let your motion wait until that time, Mr. Mason? I would like to proceed with the case as rapidly as possible."

"One of my motions can wait," Mason said. "The other one, I think, can properly be made in the presence of the jury. That is a motion to exclude all of the evidence of Mae Jordan on the ground that there is nothing in her testimony which in any way connects the defendant with any crime."

"If the Court please," Hamilton Burger said, "the witness, Dutton, will testify that one of the diamonds which was found on the underside of the desk in Perry Mason's office was one of the identical diamonds which was in the Munroe Baxter collection."

Mason said, "That doesn't connect the defendant, Duane Jefferson, with anything. Jefferson didn't give her those diamonds. Even if we are to take her testimony at face value, even if we are to concede for the sake of this motion that she took those diamonds out of the office instead of going to the office to plant diamonds, the prosecution can't bind the defendant by anything that Walter Irving did."

"It was done in his presence," Hamilton Burger said, "and as a part of a joint enterprise."

"You haven't proven either one of those points," Mason said.

Judge Hartley stroked his chin. "I am inclined to think this motion may be well taken, Mr. District Attorney. The Court has been giving this matter a great deal of thought."

"If the Court please," Hamilton Burger pleaded desperately, "I have a good case here. I have shown that these diamonds were in the possession of Munroe Baxter when he left the ship. These diamonds next show up in the possession of the defendant—"

"Not in the possession of the defendant," Mason corrected.

"In an office to which he had a key," Hamilton Burger snapped.

"The janitor had a key. The scrubwoman had a key. Walter Irving had a key."

"Exactly," Judge Hartley said. "You have to show some act of domination over those diamonds by the defendant before he can be connected with the case. That's a fundamental part of the case."

"But, Your Honor, we *have* shown that act of domination. Two of those diamonds were given to the witness Jordan to compensate her for keeping silent about her letters. We have shown that Munroe Baxter came up and took hold of that towing line which was attached to the heavy fishing rod; that the defendant stabbed him, took the belt containing the diamonds, weighted the body, then towed it away to a point where it could be dropped to the bottom."

Judge Hartley shook his head. "That is a different matter from the motion as to the testimony of Mae Jordan. However, if we are to give every credence to all of the prosecution's testimony and all inferences therefrom, as we must do in considering such a motion, there is probably an inference which will be sufficient to defeat the motion. I'll let the motion be made at this time, and reserve a ruling. Go ahead with your case, Mr. District Attorney."

Hamilton Burger put Max Dutton back on the stand.

Dutton testified that one of the gems which had been recovered from the blob of chewing gum that had been found fastened to the underside of Mason's desk was a part of the Baxter collection.

"No questions," Mason said when Hamilton Burger turned Dutton over for cross-examination.

"That," Hamilton Burger announced dramatically and unexpectedly, "finishes the People's case."

Mason said, "At this time, Your Honor, I would like to make a motion without the presence of the jury."

"The jurors will be excused for fifteen minutes," Judge Hartley said, "during which time you will remember the previous admonition of the Court."

When the jurors had filed out of court the judge nodded to Perry Mason. "Proceed with your motion."

"I move that the Court direct and instruct the jury to return a verdict of acquittal," Mason said, "on the ground that no case has been made out which would sustain a conviction, on the ground that there is no evidence tending to show a homicide, no evidence of the *corpus delicti,* and no evidence connecting the defendant with the case."

Judge Hartley said, "I am going to rule against the defense in this case, Mr. Mason. I don't want to preclude you from argument, but the Court has given this matter very careful consideration. Knowing that such a motion would be made, I want to point out to you that while, as a usual thing, proof of the *corpus delicti* includes finding the body, under the law of California that is not necessary. *Corpus delicti* means the body of the crime, not the body of the victim.

"Proof of *corpus delicti* only shows that a crime has been committed. After the crime has been committed, then it is possible to connect the defendant with that crime by proper proof.

"The *corpus delicti,* or the crime itself, like any other fact to be established in court, can be proved by circumstantial as well as direct evidence. There can be reasonable inferences deduced from the factual evidence presented.

"Now then, we have evidence which, I admit, is not very robust, which shows that Munroe Baxter, the purported victim, was carrying certain diamonds in his possession. Presumably he would not have parted from those diamonds without a struggle. Those diamonds were subsequently found under circumstances which at least support an inference that they were under the domination and in the possession of the defendant.

"One of the strongest pieces of evidence in this case is the finding of the bloodstained knife in the boat. I am free to admit that if I were a juror I would not be greatly impressed by the testimony of the witness Gilly, and yet a man who has been convicted of a felony, a man who has been convicted of perjury may well tell the truth.

"We have in this state the case of *People v. Cullen*, 37 California 2nd, 614, 234 Pacific 2nd, 1, holding that it is not essential that the body of the victim actually be found in order to support a homicide conviction.

"One of the most interesting cases ever to come before the bar of any country is the case of *Rex v. James Camb*. That was, of course, a British case, decided on Monday, April twenty-sixth, nineteen hundred and forty-eight, before the Lord Chief Justice of England.

"That is the famous *Durban Castle* case in which James Camb, a steward aboard the ship, went to the cabin of a young woman passenger. He was recognized in that cabin. The young woman disappeared and was never seen again. There was no evidence, other than circumstantial evidence, of the *corpus delicti*, save the testimony of the defendant himself admitting that he had pushed the body through the porthole but claiming that the woman was dead at the time, that she had died from natural causes and he had merely disposed of the body in that way.

"In this case we have, of course, no admission of that sort. But we do have a showing that the defendant sat in a boat, that some huge body, too big in the normal course of things to be a fish, attached itself to the heavy fishing tackle which the defendant was dangling overboard; that the defendant or the defendant's companion thereupon reached down and stabbed with a knife. A knife was subsequently found in the boat and the knife was smeared with human blood. It was the defendant's knife. I think, under the circumstances, there is enough of a case here to force the defense to meet the charge, and I think that if the jury should convict upon this evidence, the conviction would stand up."

Hamilton Burger smiled and said, "I think that if the Court will bear with us, the Court will presently see that a case of murder has been abundantly proved."

Judge Hartley looked almost suspiciously at the district attorney for a moment, then tightened his lips and said, "Very well. Call the jury."

Mason turned to his client. "This is it, Jefferson," he said. "You're going to have to go on the stand. You have not seen fit to confide in me as your lawyer. You have left me in a position where I have had to undertake the defense of your case with very little assistance from you.

"I think I can prove the witness Mae Jordan lied when she said that you came into the office while she was still there. I have the girl at the cigar counter who will testify that you men did not come in until *after* the manager of the building was standing down at the elevators. I think once we can prove that she lied in one thing, we can prove that she is to be distrusted in her entire testimony. But that young woman has made a very favorable impression on the jury."

Jefferson merely bowed in a coldly formal way. "Very well," he said.

"You have a few seconds now," Mason said. "Do you want to tell me the things that I should know?"

"Certainly," Jefferson said. "I am innocent. That is all you need to know."

"Why the devil won't you confide in me?" Mason asked.

"Because there are certain things that I am not going to tell anyone."

"In case you are interested," Mason said, "I know where

you were on the night of June fifth, and furthermore, the district attorney knows it, too."

For a moment Duane Jefferson stiffened, then he turned his face away and said indifferently, "I will answer no questions about the night of June fifth."

"You won't," Mason said, "because I'm not going to ask them on direct examination. Now just remember this one thing: I'm going to ask you where you were during the early morning hours of June sixth. You be *damn* careful that your answer doesn't ever get back of the time limit I am setting. Otherwise, the District Attorney is going to rip you to shreds. Your examination is going to be very, very brief."

"I understand."

"It will be in the nature of a gesture."

"Yes, sir, I understand."

The jury filed into the court and took their seats.

"Are you prepared to go on with you case, Mr. Mason?" Judge Hartley asked.

Mason said, "Yes, Your Honor. I won't even bother the Court and the jury by wasting time with an opening statement. I am going to rip this tissue of lies and insinuations wide open. My first witness will be Ann Riddle."

Ann Riddle, the tall, blonde girl who operated the cigar stand, came forward.

"Do you remember the occasion of the fourteenth of June of this year?"

"Yes, sir."

"Where were you at that time?"

"I was at the cigar stand in the building where you have your offices."

"Where the South African Gem Importing and Exploration Company also has its offices?"

"Yes, sir."

"You operate the cigar stand in that building?"

"Yes, sir."

"Do you remember an occasion when the manager of the

152

building came down to stand at the elevator with a young woman?"

"Yes, sir."

"Did you see the defendant at that time?"

"Yes, sir. The defendant and Mr. Irving, his associate, were returning from lunch. They—"

"Now just a minute," Mason said. "You don't *know* they were returning from lunch."

"No, sir."

"All right, please confine your statements to what happened."

"Well, they were entering the building. The manager was standing there. One of the men—I think it was Mr. Irving, but I can't remember for sure—started to walk over to the manager of the building, then saw that he was intent upon something else, so he turned away. The two men entered the elevator."

"This was after the alarm had been given about the burglary?" Mason asked.

"Yes, sir."

"You may inquire," Mason said to Hamilton Burger.

Hamilton Burger smiled. "I have no questions."

"I will call the defendant, Duane Jefferson, to the stand," Mason said.

Duane Jefferson, cool and calm, got up and walked slowly to the witness stand. For a moment he didn't look at the jury, then when he did deign to glance at them, it was with an air of superiority bordering on contempt. "The damn fool!" Mason whispered under his breath.

Hamilton Burger tilted back in his swivel chair, he interlaced his fingers back of his head, winked at one of his deputies, and a broad smile suffused his face.

"Did you kill Munroe Baxter?" Mason asked.

"No, sir."

"Did you know that those diamonds were in your office?"

"No, sir."

"Where were you on the morning of the sixth of June?

I'll put it this way, where were you from 2:00 A.M. on the sixth of June to noon of that day?"

"During the times mentioned I was in my apartment, sleeping, until a little after seven. Then I had breakfast with my associate, Walter Irving. After breakfast we went to the office."

"Cross-examine," Mason snapped viciously at Hamilton Burger.

Hamilton Burger said, "I will be very brief. I have only a couple of questions, Mr. Jefferson. Have *you* ever been convicted of a felony?"

"I—" Suddenly Jefferson seemed to collapse in the witness chair.

"Have you?" Hamilton Burger thundered.

"I made one mistake in my life," Jefferson said. "I have tried to live it down. I thought I had."

"Did you, indeed?" Hamilton Burger said scornfully. "Where were you convicted, Mr. Jefferson?"

"In New York."

"You served time in Sing Sing?"

"Yes."

"Under the name of Duane Jefferson?"

"No, sir."

"Under what name?"

"Under the name of James Kincaid."

"Exactly," Hamiltion Burger said. "You were convicted of larceny by trick and device."

"Yes."

"You posed as an English heir, did you not? And you told—"

"Objected to," Mason said. "Counsel has no right to amplify the admission."

"Sustained."

"Were you, at one time, known as 'Gentleman Jim,' a nickname of the underworld?"

"Objected to," Mason said.

"Sustained."

Hamilton Burger said scornfully, "I will ask no further questions."

As one in a daze, the defendant stumbled from the stand.

Mason said, his lips a hard, white line, "Mr. Walter Irving take the stand."

The bailiff called, "Walter Irving."

When there was no response, the call was taken up in the corridors.

Paul Drake came forward, beckoned to Mason. "He's skipped, Perry. He was sitting near the door. He took it on the lam the minute Burger asked Jefferson about his record. Good Lord! What a mess! What a lousy mess!"

Judge Hartley said not unkindly, "Mr. Irving doesn't seem to be present, Mr. Mason. Was he under subpoena?"

"Yes, Your Honor."

"Do you wish the Court to issue a bench warrant?"

"No, Your Honor," Mason said. "Perhaps Mr. Irving had his reasons for leaving."

"I daresay he did," Hamilton Burger said sarcastically.

"That's the defendant's case," Mason said. "We rest."

It was impossible for Hamilton Burger to keep the gloating triumph out of his voice. "I will," he said, "call only three witnesses on rebuttal. The first is Mrs. Agnes Elmer."

Mrs. Agnes Elmer gave her name and address. She was, she explained, the manager of the apartment house where the defendant, Duane Jefferson, had rented an apartment shortly after his arrival in the city.

"Directing your attention to the early morning of June sixth," Hamilton Burger said, "do you know whether Duane Jefferson was in his apartment?"

"I do."

"Was he in that apartment?"

"He was not."

"Was his bed slept in that night?"

"It was not."

"Cross-examine," Hamilton Burger said.

Mason, recognizing that the short, direct examination was intended to bait a trap into which he must walk on cross-examination, flexed his arms slowly, as though stretching with weariness, said, "How do you fix the date, Mrs. Elmer?"

"A party rang up shortly before midnight on the fifth," Mrs. Elmer said. "It was a woman's voice. She told me it was absolutely imperative that she get in touch with Mr. Jefferson. She said Mr. Jefferson had got her in—"

"Just a minute," Mason interrupted. "I object, Your Honor, to this witness relating any conversations which occurred outside of the presence of the the the defendant."

"Oh, Your Honor," Hamilton Burger said. "This is plainly admissible. Counsel asked this question himself. He asked her how she fixed the date. She's telling him."

Judge Hartley said, "There may be some technical merit to your contention, Mr. District Attorney, but this is a court of justice, not a place for a legal sparring match. The whole nature of your examination shows you had carefully baited this as a trap for the cross-examiner. I'm going to sustain the objection. You can make your own case by your own witness.

"Now, the Court is going to ask the witness if there is any other way you can fix the date, any way, that is, depending on your own actions."

"Well," the witness said, "I know it was the sixth because that was the day I went to the dentist. I had a terrific toothache that night and couldn't sleep."

"And how do you fix the date that you went to the dentist?" Mason asked.

"From the dentist's appointment book."

"So you don't know of your own knowledge what date you went to the dentist, only the date that is shown in the dentist's book?"

"That's right."

"And the entry of that date in the dentist's book was not made in your own handwriting. In other words, you have used a conversation with the dentist to refresh your memory."

"Well, I asked him what date I came in, and he consulted his records and told me."

"Exactly," Mason said. "But you don't know of your own knowledge how he kept his records."

"Well, he's supposed to keep them—"

Mason smiled. "But *you* have no independent recollection of anything except that it was the night that you had the toothache, is that right?"

"Well, if you'd had that toothache—"

"I'm asking you if that's the only way you can fix the date, that it was the night you had the toothache?"

"Yes."

"And then, at the request of the district attorney, you tried to verify the date?"

"Yes."

"When did the district attorney request that you do that?"

"I don't know. It was late in the month sometime."

"And did you go to the dentist's office, or did you telephone him?"

"I telephoned him."

"And asked him the date when you had your appointment?"

"Yes."

"Aside from that, you wouldn't have been able to tell whether it had been the sixth, the seventh, or the eighth?"

"I suppose not."

"So you have refreshed your recollection by taking the word of someone else. In other words, the testimony you are now giving as to the date is purely hearsay evidence?"

"Oh, Your Honor," Hamilton Burger said, "I think this witness has the right to refresh her recollection by—"

Judge Hartley shook his head. "The witness has testified that she can't remember the date except by fixing it in connection with other circumstances, and those other circumstances which she is using to refresh her recollection depend upon the unsworn testimony of another. Quite plainly hearsay testimony, Mr. District Attorney."

Hamilton Burger bowed. "Very well, Your Honor."

"That's all," Mason said.

"Call Josephine Carter," Burger said.

Josephine Carter was sworn, testified she was a switchboard operator at the apartment house where the defendant had his apartment, that she worked from 10:00 P.M. on the night of the fifth of June until 6:00 A.M. on the morning of June sixth.

"Did you ring the defendant's phone that night?"

"Yes."

"When?"

"Shortly before midnight. I was told it was an emergency and I—"

"Never mind what you were *told*. What did you *do*?"

"I rang the phone."

"Did you get an answer?"

"No. The party who was calling left a message and asked me to keep calling to see that Mr. Jefferson got that message as soon as he came in."

"How often did you continue to ring?"

"Every hour."

"Until when?"

"When I went off duty at six in the morning."

"Did you ever get an answer?"

"No."

"From your desk at the switchboard can you watch the corridor to the elevator, and did you thereafter watch to see if the defendant came in?"

"Yes. I kept watch so as to call to him when he came in."

"He didn't come in while you were on duty?"

"No."

"You're certain?"

"Positive."

"Cross-examine," Burger snapped at Mason.

"How did you know the phone was ringing?" Mason asked smilingly.

"Why I depressed the key."

"Phones get out of order occasionally?"

"Yes."

"Is there any check signal on the board by which you can tell if the phone is ringing?"

"You get a peculiar sound when the phone rings, sort of a hum."

"And if the phone doesn't ring, do you get that hum?"

"I . . . we haven't been troubled that way."

"Do you know of your own knowledge that you fail to get that hum when the phone is not ringing?"

"That's the way the board is supposed to work."

"I'm asking you if you know of your own knowledge?"

"Well, Mr. Mason, I have never been in an apartment where the phone was not ringing and at the same time been downstairs at the switchboard trying to ring that telephone."

"Exactly," Mason said. "That's the point I was trying to make, Miss Carter. That's all."

"Just a moment," Hamilton Burger said. "I have one question on redirect. Did you keep an eye on the persons who went in and out, to see if Mr. Jefferson came in?"

"I did."

"Is your desk so located that you could have seen him when he came in?"

"Yes. Everyone who enters the apartment has to walk down a corridor, and I can see through a glass door into that corridor."

"That's all," Burger said, smiling.

"I have one or two questions on recross-examination," Mason said. "I'll only bother you for a moment, Miss Carter. You have now stated that you kept looking up whenever anyone came in, to see if the defendant came in."

"Yes, sir."

"And you could have seen him if he had come in?"

"Yes, sir. Very easily. From my station at the switchboard I can watch people who come down the corridor."

"So you want the Court and the jury to understand that you are certain the defendant didn't come in during the time you were on duty?"

"Well, he didn't come in from the time I first rang his telephone until I quit ringing it at six o'clock, when I went off duty."

"And what time did you first ring his telephone?"

"It was before midnight, perhaps eleven o'clock, perhaps a little after eleven."

"And then what?"

"Then I rang two or three times between the time of the first call and one o'clock, and then after 1:00 A.M. I made it a point to ring every hour on the hour."

"Just short rings or—"

"No, I rang several long rings each time."

"And after your first ring around midnight you were satisfied the defendant was not in his apartment?"

"Yes, sir."

"And because you were watching the corridor you were satisfied that he couldn't have entered the house and gone to his apartment without your seeing him?"

"Yes, sir."

"Then why," Mason asked, "if you *knew* he wasn't in his apartment and *knew* that he hadn't come in, did you keep on ringing the telephone at hourly intervals?"

The witness looked at Mason, started to say something, stopped, blinked her eyes, said, "Why, I . . . I . . . I don't know. I just did it."

"In other words," Mason said, "you *thought* there was a possibility he might have come in without your seeing him?"

"Well, of course, that *could* have happened."

"Then when you just now told the district attorney that it would have been impossible for the defendant to have come in without your seeing him, you were mistaken?"

"I . . . well, I . . . I had talked it over with the district attorney and . . . well, I thought that's what I was supposed to say."

"Exactly," Mason said, smiling. "Thank you."

Josephine Carter looked at Hamilton Burger to see if there were any more questions, but Hamilton Burger was making a great show of pawing through some papers. "That's all," he snapped gruffly.

Josephine Carter left the witness stand.

"I will now call Ruth Dickey," Hamilton Burger said.

Ruth Dickey came forward, was sworn, and testified that she was and had been on the fourteenth of June an elevator operator in the building where the South African Gem Importing and Exploration Company had its offices.

"Did you see Duane Jefferson, the defendant in this case, on the fourteenth of June a little after noon?"

"Yes, sir."

"When?"

"Well, he and Mr. Irving, his associate, rode down in the elevator with me about ten minutes past twelve. The defendant said he was going to lunch."

"When did they come back?"

"They came back about five minutes to one and rode up in the elevator with me."

"Did anything unusual happen on that day?"

"Yes, sir."

"What?"

"The manager of the building and one of the stenographers got into the elevator with me, and the manager asked me to run right down to the street floor because it was an emergency."

"Was this before or after the defendant and Irving had gone up with you?"

"After."

"You're certain?"

"Yes."

"About how long after?"

"At least five minutes."

"How well do you know the defendant?" Hamilton Burger asked.

"I have talked with him off and on."

"Have you ever been out with him socially?"

She lowered her eyes. "Yes."

"Now, did the defendant make any statements to you with reference to his relationship with Ann Riddle, the young woman who operates the cigar stand?"

"Yes. He said that he and his partner had set her up in

business, that she was a lookout for them, but that no one else knew the connection. He said if I'd be nice to him, he could do something for me, too."

"You may cross-examine," Hamilton Burger said.

"You have had other young men take you out from time to time?" Mason asked.

"Well, yes."

"And quite frequently you have had them make rather wild promises about what they could do about setting you up in business if you would only be nice to them?"

She laughed. "I'll say," she said. "You'd be surprised about what some of them say."

"I dare say I would," Mason said. "That's all. Thank you, Miss Dickey."

"That's all our rebuttal," Hamilton Burger said.

Judge Hartley's voice was sympathetic. "I know that it is customary to have a recess before arguments start, but I would like very much to get this case finished today. I think that we can at least start the argument, unless there is some reason for making a motion for a continuance."

Mason, tight-lipped, shook his head. "Let's go ahead with it," he said.

"Very well, Mr. District Attorney, you may make your opening argument."

Chapter 18

Hamilton Burger's argument to the jury was relatively short. It was completed within an hour after court reconvened following the noon recess. It was a masterpiece of forensic eloquence, of savage triumph, of a bitter, vindictive attack on the defendant and by implication on his attorney.

Mason's argument, which followed, stressed the point that while perjurers and waterfront scum had made an attack on his client, no one had yet shown that Munroe Baxter was murdered. Munroe Baxter, Mason insisted, could show up alive and well at any time, without having contradicted the testimony of any witness.

Hamilton Burger's closing argument was directed to the fact that the Court would instruct the jury that *corpus delicti* could be shown by circumstantial evidence, as well as by direct evidence. It was an argument which took only fifteen minutes.

The Court read instructions to the jurors, who retired to the jury room for their deliberations.

Mason, in the courtroom, his face a cold, hard mask, thoughtfully paced the floor.

Della Street, sitting at the counsel table, gave him her silent sympathy. Paul Drake, who had for once been too depressed even to try to eat, sat with his head in his hands.

Mason glanced at the clock, sighed wearily, ceased his pacing and dropped into a chair.

"Any chance, Perry?" Paul Drake asked.

Mason shook his head. "Not with the evidence in this shape. My client is a dead duck. Any luck with this car rental?"

"No luck at all, Perry. We've covered every car rental agency here and in outlying towns where they have branches."

Mason was thoughtful for a moment. "What about Walter Irving?"

"Irving has flown the coop," Drake said. "He left the courtroom, climbed into a taxicab and vanished. This time my men knew what he was going to try to do, and they were harder to shake. But within an hour he had had ditched the shadows. It was a hectic hour."

"How did he do it?"

"It was very simple," Drake said. "Evidently it was part of a prearranged scheme. He had chartered a helicopter that was waiting for him at one of the outlying airports. He drove out there, got in the helicopter and took off."

"Can't you find out what happened? Don't they have to file some sort of a flight plan or—"

"Oh, we know what happened well enough," Drake said. "He chartered the helicopter to take him to the International Airport. Halfway there, he changed his mind and talked the helicopter into landing at the Santa Monica Airport. A rented car was waiting there."

"He's gone?"

"Gone slick and clean. We'll probably pick up his trail later on, but it isn't going to be easy, and by that time it won't do any good."

Mason thought for a moment. Suddenly he sat bolt upright. "Paul," he said, "we've overlooked a bet!"

"What?"

"A person renting a car has to show his driving license?"

"That's right."

"You've been looking for car rentals in the name of Marline Chaumont?"

"That's right."

"All right," Mason said. "Start your men looking for car rentals in the name of Walter Irving. Call your men on the phone. Start a network of them making a search. I want that information, and I want it now."

Drake, seemingly glad to be able to leave the depressing atmosphere of the courtroom, said, "Okay, I'll start right away, Perry."

Shortly before five o'clock a buzzer announced that the jury had reached its verdict. The jury was brought into court and the verdict was read by the foreman.

"We, the jury impaneled to try the above-entitled case, find the defendant guitly of murder in the first degree."

There was no recommendation for life imprisonment or leniency.

Judge Hartley's eyes were sympathetic as he looked at Perry Mason. "Can we agree upon having the Court fix a time for pronouncing sentence?" he asked.

"I would like an early date for hearing a motion for a new trial," Mason said. "I will stipulate that Friday will be satisfactory for presenting a motion for new trial and fixing sentence. We will waive the question of time."

"How about the district attorney's office?" Judge Hartley asked. "Will Friday be satisfactory?"

The deputy district attorney, who sat at the counsel table, said, "Well, Your Honor, I think it will be all right. Mr. Burger is in conference with the press at the moment. He—"

"He asked you to represent the district attorney's office?" Judge Hartley asked.

"Yes, Your Honor."

"Represent it then," Judge Hartley said shortly. "Is Friday satisfactory?"

"Yes, Your Honor."

"Friday morning at ten o'clock," Judge Hartley said. "Court is adjourned. The defendant is remanded to custody."

Reporters, who usually swarmed about Perry Mason asking for a statement, were now closeted with Hamilton Burger. The few spectators who had been interested enough to await the verdict got up and went home. Mason picked up his brief case. Della Street tucked her hand through his arm, gave him a reassuring squeeze. "You warned him, Chief," she said. "Not once, but a dozen times. He had it coming."

Mason merely nodded. Paul Drake, hurrying down the corridor, said, "I've got something, Perry."

"Did you hear the verdict?" Mason asked.

Paul Drake's eyes refused to meet Mason's. "I heard it."

"What have you got?" Mason asked.

"Walter Irving rented an automobile the day that Marline Chaumont disappeared from the airport. Last night he rented another one."

"I thought so," Mason said. "Has he turned back the first automobile?"

"No."

"He keeps the rental paid?"

"Yes."

"We can't get him on the ground of embezzling the automobile, so we can have police looking for it as a 'hot' car?"

"Apparently not."

Mason turned to Della Street. "Della, you have a shorthand book in your purse?"

She nodded.

"All right," Mason said to Paul Drake, "let's go, Paul."

"Where?" Drake asked.

"To see Ann Riddle, the girl who bought the cigar counter in our building," Mason said. "We may be able to get to her before she, too, flies the coop. Hamilton Burger is too busy with the press, decorating himself with floral wreaths, to do much thinking now."

Drake his voice sympathetic, said, "Gosh, Perry, it's . . . I can imagine how you feel . . . having a client convicted of first-degree murder. It's the first time you've every had a client convicted in a murder case."

Mason turned to Paul Drake, his eyes were cold and hard. "My client," he said, "hasn't been convicted of anything."

For a moment Drake acted as if his ears had betrayed

him, then, at something he saw in Mason's face, he refrained from asking questions.

"Get the address of that girl who bought the cigar stand," Mason said, "and let's go."

Chapter 19

Mason, his face implacably determined, scorned the chair offered him by the frightened blonde.

"You can talk now," he said, "or you can talk later. Whichever you want. If you talk now it may do you some good. If you talk later you're going to be convicted as an accessory in a murder case. Make up your mind."

"I've nothing to say."

Mason said, "Irving and Jefferson went into the building *before* the excitement. When they entered their office, Mae Jordan was there. They caught her. The phone rang. They were warned that the police had been notified that a girl was breaking into the office and that the police were coming up; that the girl who had seen the woman breaking in and the manager of the building were waiting at the elevators. There was only one person who could have given them that information. That was you."

"You have no right to say that."

"I've said it," Mason said, "and I'm saying it again. The next time I say it, it's going to be in open court.

"By tomorrow morning at ten o'clock we'll have torn into your past and will have found out all about the connection between you and Irving. By that time it'll be too late for you to do anything. You've committed perjury. We're putting a tail on you. Now start talking."

Under the impact of Mason's gaze she at first averted her eyes, then restlessly shifted her position in the chair.

"Start talking," Mason said.

"I don't have to answer to you. You're not the police. You—"

"Start talking."

"All right," she said. "I was paid to keep a watch on things, to telephone them if anything suspicious happened. There's nothing unlawful about that."

"It goes deeper than that," Mason said. "You were in on the whole thing. It was their money that put you in the cigar store. What's your connection with this thing?"

"You can't prove any of that. That's a false and slanderous statement. Duane Jefferson never told that little tramp anything like that. If he did, it was false."

"Start talking," Mason said.

She hesitated, then stubbornly shook her head.

Mason motioned to Della Street. "Go over to the telephone, Della. Ring up Homicide Squad. Get Lieutenant Tragg on the line. Tell him I want to talk with him."

Della Street started for the telephone.

"Now wait a minute," the blonde said hurriedly. "You can't—"

"Can't what?" Mason asked as her voice trailed into silence.

"Can't make anything stick on me. You haven't got any proof."

"I'm getting it," Mason told her. "Paul Drake here is an expert detective. He has men on the job right now, men who are concentrating on what you and Irving were doing."

"All right. Suppose my gentleman friend *did* loan me the money to buy a cigar stand. There's nothing wrong with that. I'm over the age of consent. I can do what I damn please."

Mason said, "This is your last chance. Walter Irving is putting out a lot of false clues, shaking off any possible pursuit. Then he'll go to Marline Chaumont. She's in one of the outlying towns. When she and Irving get together, something's going to happen. He must have given you an address where you could reach him in case of any emergency. That will be Marline's hide-out. Where is it?"

She shook her head.

Mason nodded to Della Street. Della Street started putting through the call.

Abruptly the blonde began to cry.

"I want Homicide Department, please," Della Street said into the phone.

The blonde said, "It's in Santa Ana."

"Where?" Mason asked.

She fumbled with her purse, took out an address, handed it to Mason. Mason nodded, and Della Street hung up the telephone.

"Come on," Mason said.

"What do you mean, come on?" the girl said.

"You heard me," Mason told her. "We're not leaving you behind to make any telephone calls. This is too critical for us to botch it up now."

"You can't *make* me go!"

"I can't make you go with *me,* but I can damn sure see that you're locked up in the police station. The only bad thing is that will cost about fifteen minutes. Which do you want?"

She said, "Stop looking at me like that. You frighten me. You—"

"I'm putting it to you cold turkey," Mason said. "Do you want to take a murder rap or not?"

"I—" She hesitated.

"Get your things on," Mason said.

Ann Riddle moved toward the closet.

"Watch her, Della," Mason said. "We don't want her to pick up any weapons."

Ann Riddle put on a light coat, picked up her purse. Paul Drake looked in the purse and made sure there was no weapon in it.

The four of them went down in the elevator, wordlessly got in Mason's car. Mason tooled the car out to the freeway, gathered speed.

Chapter 20

The house was in a quiet residential district. A light was on in the living room. A car was parked in the garage. A wet strip on the sidewalk showed that the lawn had recently been sprinkled.

Mason parked the car, jerked open the door, strode up the steps to the porch. Della Street hurried along behind him. Paul Drake kept a hand on the arm of Ann Riddle.

Mason rang the bell.

The door opened half an inch. "Who is it?" a woman's voice asked.

Mason pushed his weight against the door so suddenly that the door was pushed inward.

Marline Chaumont, staggering back, regarded Mason with frightened eyes. "You!" she said.

"We came to get your brother," Mason said.

"My brother is—how you call it?—sick in the upstairs. He has flies in his belfry. He cannot be disturbed. He is asleep."

"Wake him up," Mason said.

"But you cannot do this. My brother he— You are not the law, *non*?"

"No," Mason said. "But we'll have the law here in about five minutes."

Marline Chaumont's face contorted into a spasm of anger. "You!" she spat at the blonde. "You had to pull a double cross!"

"I didn't," Ann Riddle said. "I only—"

"I know what you did, you double-crosser!" Marline Chaumont said. "I spit on you. You stool squab!"

"Never mind that," Mason said. "Where's the man you claim is your brother?"

"But he *is* my brother!"

"Phooey," Mason told her.

"He was taken from the hospital—"

"The man who was taken from the state hospital," Mason said, "isn't related to you any more than I am. You used him only as a prop. I don't know what you've done with him. Put him in a private institution somewhere, I suppose. I want the man who's taken his place, and I want him now."

"You are crazy in the head yourself," Marline Chaumont said. "You have no right to—"

"Take care of her, Paul," Mason said, and started marching down the hall toward the back of the house.

"You'll be killed!" she screamed. "You cannot do this. You—"

Mason tried the doors one at a time. The third door opened into a bedroom. A man, thin and emaciated, was lying on the bed, his hands handcuffed at the wrists.

A big, burly individual who had been reading a magazine got slowly to his feet. "What the hell!" he thundered.

Mason sized him up. "You look like an ex-cop to me," he said.

"What's it to you?" the man asked.

"Probably retired," Mason said. "Hung out your shingle as a private detective. Didn't do so well. Then this job came along."

"Say, what're you talking about?"

"I don't know what story they told *you*," Mason said, "and I don't know whether you're in on it or not, but whatever they told you, the jig's up. I'm Perry Mason, the lawyer."

The man who was handcuffed on the bed turned to Perry Mason. His eyes, dulled with sedatives, seemed to be having some difficulty getting in focus.

"Who are you?" he asked in the thick voice of a sleep talker.

Mason said, "I've come to take you out of here."

The bodyguard said, "This man's a mental case. He's inclined to be violent. He can't be released and he has delusions—"

"I know," Mason said. "His real name is Pierre Chaumont. He keeps thinking he's someone else. He has a delusion that his real name is—"

"Say, how do you know all this?" the bodyguard asked.

Mason said, "They gave you a steady job. A woman handed you a lot of soft soap, and you probably think she's one of the sweetest, most wonderful women on earth. It's time you woke up. As for this man on the bed, he's going with me right now. First we're going to the best doctor we can find, and then . . . well, then we'll get ready to keep a date on Friday morning at ten o'clock.

"You can either be in jail at that time or a free man. Make your choice now. We're separating the men from the boys. If you're in on this thing all the way, you're in a murder case. If you were just hired to act as a guard for a man who is supposed to be a mental case, that's something else. You have your opportunity to make your decision right now. There's a detective downstairs and police are on their way out. They'll be here within a matter of minutes. They'll want to know where you stand. I'm giving you your chance right now, and it's your *last* chance."

The big guard blinked his eyes slowly. "You say this man *isn't* a mental case?"

"Of course he isn't."

"I've seen the papers. He was taken from a state hospital."

"Some other guy was taken from a state hospital," Mason said, "and then they switched patients. This isn't a debating society. Make up your mind."

"You're Perry Mason, the lawyer?"

"That's right."

"Got any identification on you?"

Mason handed the man his card, showed him his driving license.

The guard sighed. "Okay," he said. "You win."

Chapter 21

The bailiff called court to order.

Hamilton Burger, his face wearing a look of smug satisfaction, beamed about the courtroom.

Judge Hartley said, "This is the time fixed for hearing a motion for new trial and for pronouncing judgment in the case of *People* v. *Duane Jefferson*. Do you wish to be heard, Mr. Mason?"

"Yes, Your Honor," Perry Mason said. "I move for a new trial of the case on the ground that the trial took place in the absence of the defendant."

"What?" Hamilton Burger shouted. "The defendant was present in court every minute of the time! The records so show."

"Will you stand up, Mr. Duane Jefferson?" Mason asked.

The man beside Mason stood up. Another man seated near the middle of the courtroom also stood up. Judge Hartley looked at the man in the courtroom.

"Come forward," Mason said.

"Just a minute," Judge Hartley said. "What's the meaning of this, Mr. Mason?"

"I asked Mr. Jefferson to stand up."

"He's standing up," Hamilton Burger said.

"Exactly," Mason said.

"Who's this other man?" the Court asked. "Is he a witness?"

"He's Duane Jefferson," Mason said.

"Now, just a minute, just a minute," Hamilton Burger said. "What's all this about, what kind of a flim-flam is

175

counsel trying to work here? Let's get this thing straight. Here's the defendant standing here within the bar."

"And here's Duane Jefferson coming forward," Mason said. "I am moving for a new trial on the ground that the entire trial of Duane Jefferson for first-degree murder took place in his absense."

"Now just a moment, just a moment!" Hamilton Burger shouted. "I might have known there would be something like this. Counsel can't confuse the issues. It doesn't make any difference now whether this man is Duane Jefferson or whether he's John Doe. He's the man who committed the murder. He's the man who was seen committing the murder. He's the man who was tried for the murder. If he went under the name of Duane Jefferson, that isn't going to stop him from being sentenced for the murder."

"But," Mason said, "some of your evidence was directed against my client, Duane Jefferson."

"*Your* client?" Hamilton Burger said. "That's your client standing next to you."

Mason smiled and shook his head. "*This* is my client," he said, beckoning to the man standing at the gate of the bar to come forward once more. "This is Duane Jefferson. He's the one I was retained to represent by the South African Gem Importing and Exploration Company."

"Well, he's not the one you defended," Hamilton Burger said. "You can't get out of the mess this way."

Mason smiled and said, "I'm defending him now."

"Go ahead and defend him. He isn't accused of anything!"

"And I'm moving for a new trial on the ground that the trial took place in the absence of the defendant."

"This is the defendant standing right here!" Hamilton Burger insisted. "The trial took place in *his* presence. *He's* the one who was convicted. I don't care what you do with this other man, regardless of what his name is."

"Oh, but you introduced evidence consisting of articles belonging to the real Duane Jefferson," Mason said. "That dagger, for instance. The contents of the letters."

"What do you mean?"

"Mae W. Jordan told all about the letters she had received from Duane Jefferson, about the contents of those letters. I moved to strike out her testimony. The motion was denied. The testimony went to the jury about the Daddy Longlegs letters, about the Prince Charming letters, about the gag photographs, about the getting acquainted, and about the dagger."

"Now, just a moment," Judge Hartley said. "The Court will bear with you for a moment in this matter, Mr. Mason, but the Court is going to resort to stern measures if it appears this is some dramatic presentation of a technicality which you are using to dramatize the issues."

"I'm trying to clarify the issues," Mason said. "What happened is very simple. Duane Jefferson, who is standing there by the mahogany swinging gate which leads to the interior of the bar, is a trusted employee of the South African Gem Importing and Exploration Company. He was sent to this country in the company of Walter Irving of the Paris office to open a branch office. They were to receive half a million dollars' worth of diamonds in the mail.

"Walter Irving, who had been gambling heavily, was deeply involved and knew that very shortly after he had left Paris there would be an audit of the books and his defalcations would be discovered.

"This man, James Kincaid, was groomed to take the place of Duane Jefferson. After the shipment of gems was received, James Kincaid would take the gems and disappear. Walter Irving would duly report an embezzlement by Jefferson and thereafter Jefferson's body would be discovered under such circumstances that it would appear he had committed suicide.

"The trouble was that they couldn't let well enough alone. They knew that Munroe Baxter was smuggling diamonds into the country, and they decided to kill Baxter and get the gems. Actually, Walter Irving had been working with Baxter in connection with the smuggling and for a fee had arranged for the stones to be delivered to Baxter under such circumstances that they could be smuggled into this country.

"The spurious Duane Jefferson didn't need to be clever about it, because he intended to have the shipment of stones in his possession and the real Duane Jefferson's body found, long before the police could make an investigation. However, because of a tax situation, the shipment of gems was delayed, and naturally they couldn't afford to have the spurious Jefferson disappear until the shipment had been received, so that Walter Irving could then report the defalcation to the company. Therefore, the real Duane Jefferson had to be kept alive."

"Your Honor, Your Honor!" Hamilton Burger shouted. "This is simply another one of those wild-eyed, dramatic grandstands for which counsel is so noted. This time his client has been convicted of first-degree murder, and I intend to see to it personally that his client pays the supreme penalty."

Mason pointed to the man standing in the aisle. "This is my client," he said. "This is the man I was retained to represent. I intend to show that his trial took place in his absence. Come forward and be sworn, Mr. Jefferson."

"Your Honor, I object!" Hamilton Burger shouted. "I object to any such procedure. I insist that this defendant is the only defendant before the Court."

Judge Hartley said, "Now, just a moment. I want to get to the bottom of this thing, and I want to find out exactly what counsel's contention is before I start making any rulings. Court will take an adjournment for fifteen minutes while we try to get at the bottom of this thing. I will ask counsel for both sides to meet me in chambers. The defendant, in the meantime, is in custody. He will remain in custody."

Mason grinned.

The tall, gaunt man standing in the aisle turned back toward the audience. Mae Jordan moved toward him.

"Hello, Prince Charming," she ventured somewhat dubiously. Jefferson's eyes lit up.

"Hello, Lady Guinevere," he said in a low voice. "I was told you'd be here."

"Prince . . . Prince Charming!"

Mason said, "I'll leave him in your custody, Miss Jordan." Then Mason marched into the judge's chambers."

Chapter 22

"Well?" Judge Hartley said.

"It was quite a plot," Mason explained. "Actually, it was hatched in Paris as soon as Walter Irving knew he was going to be sent over to assist Duane Jefferson in opening the new office. A girl named Marline Chaumont, who had been a Paris party girl for the company and who knew her way around, was in on it. James Kincaid was in on it. They would have gotten away with the whole scheme, if it hadn't been for the fact that they were too eager. They knew that Baxter was planning to smuggle in three hundred thousand dollars' worth of diamonds. Gilly was to have taken the fishing boat out and made the delivery. They persuaded Gilly that Baxter had changed his mind at the last minute because of Gilly's record. He wanted these other men to take the boat out. Gilly was lying when he testified about his rental for the boat. He received twenty-five hundred dollars. That was the agreed price. Marline Chaumont has given me a sworn statement."

"Now just a minute," Judge Hartley said. "Are you now making this statement about the client you're representing in court?"

"I'm not representing him in court," Mason said. "I'm representing the real Duane Jefferson. That's the one I was retained to represent. I would suggest, however, that the Court give this other man an opportunity to get counsel of his own, or appoint counsel to represent him. He, too, is entitled to a new trial."

"He can't get a new trial," Hamilton Burger roared, "even if what you say is true. You defended him and you lost the case."

Mason smiled coldly at Hamilton Burger. "You might have made that stick," he said, "if it hadn't been for the testimony of Mae Jordan about all of her correspondence with Duane Jefferson. That correspondence was with the real Duane Jefferson, not with the man you are trying for murder. You can't convict Duane Jefferson of anything, because he wasn't present during his trial. You can't make the present conviction stick against the defendant now in court, because you used evidence that related to the real Duane Jefferson, not to him.

"What you should have done was to have checked your identification of the man you had under arrest. You were so damned anxious to get something on me that when you found from his fingerprints that he had a record, you let your enthusiasm run away with you.

"You let Mae Jordan testify to a lot of things that had happened between her and the real Duane Jefferson. It never occurred to you to make certain that the man she sent the knife to was the same man you were trying for murder.

"The spurious Jefferson and Irving drugged the real Jefferson shortly after they left Chicago on the train. They stole all of his papers, stole the Jordan letters, stole the knife. It will be up to you to prove that at the next trial—and I'm not going to help you. You can go get the evidence yourself. However, I have Marline Chaumont in my office and I have a sworn statement made by her, which I now hand to the Court, with a copy for the district attorney.

"Just one suggestion, though. If you ever want to tie this case up, you'd better find out who that man was who was in the boat with Kincaid, because it certainly wasn't Irving."

"And now may I ask the Court to relieve me of any responsibility in the matter of the defendant, James Kincaid, who is out there in the courtroom. He tricked me into appearing in court for him by artifice, fraud, and by misrepresenting his identity. My only client is Duane Jefferson."

"I think," Judge Hartley said, "I want to talk with this

Duane Jefferson. I suppose you can establish his identity beyond any question, Mr. Mason?"

"His fingerprints were taken in connection with his military service," Mason said.

"That should be good enough evidence," Judge Hartley agreed, smiling. "I'd like to have a talk with him now."

Mason got up, walked to the door of chambers, looked out at the courtroom, and turned back to smile at the judge. "I guess I'll have to interrupt him," Mason said. "He and the witness Mae Jordan are jabbering away like a house afire. There seems to be a sort of common understanding between them. I guess it's because they're both interested in photography."

Judge Hartley's smile had broadened. "Perhaps, Mr. Mason," he suggested tentatively, "Miss Jordan is telling Mr. Jefferson where she got that key."